Crown Witness

CROWN
WITNESS

GILLIAN LINSCOTT

St. Martin's Press
New York

Library of Congress Cataloging-in-Publication Data

Linscott, Gillian.
Crown witness / Gillian Linscott.
p. cm.
ISBN 0-312-13456-8
1. George, V, King of Great Britain, 1865–1936—
Assassination attempts—Fiction.   2. George, V, King of
Great Britain, 1865–1936—Coronation—Fiction.
3. Bray, Nell (Fictitious character)—Fiction.
4. Women detectives—England—Fiction.   I. Title.
PR6062.I54C76   1995
823'.914—dc20   95-34759   CIP

First published in Great Britain by
Little, Brown and Company

First U.S. Edition: December 1995
10 9 8 7 6 5 4 3 2 1

Crown Witness

ONE

'NELL, HAVE YOU ... ?'

For the past half-hour Jessie had been trying to ask me something, but she'd been interrupted every time. We were in a small side room of our headquarters at 4 Clement's Inn, sharing it with a bundle of purple and green pennants on poles, a failed early design for Queen Elizabeth's wig and three assistants to the parade Chief Marshal, all three in an even.worse state than the wig. It was late on the evening of Friday 16 June and outside dusk was settling over a London made hectic and over excited by the near prospect of the coronation of King George V. You might have expected the Women's Social and Political Union to be immune from coronation fever, but we'd invented our own version. We were organising a Women's Coronation Procession intended, according to our advance billing, to be 'the greatest Procession of Women that has ever been seen since the world began', on the evening of the Saturday before the coronation, from the Thames Embankment to a rally in the Royal Albert Hall. Five miles of marchers representing the achievements of women from the medieval abbesses to the present day.

Before Jessie could complete the question yet another anxious messenger arrived.

'The gymnastic teachers want to march swinging their Indian clubs but the London mistresses say they won't stand for it.'

A glance at the order of procession, pinned on the

1

wall behind us, made this comprehensible. The Gymnastic Teachers' Suffrage Society, marching behind a band towards the end of the procession, would be followed by other teachers, including the London Mistresses' Union. Having seen the gymnastic teachers doing club drill in the past, I could understand their anxiety. Jessie was decisive.

'Definitely no Indian clubs. If they hit someone in the crowd we're bound to be accused of doing it on purpose and we don't want trouble tomorrow.'

Don't want trouble. If the Women's Coronation Procession had a motto, that would be it. Never mind the fact that only a few months ago the police had broken up one of our demonstrations outside Parliament in a pitched battle that left cracked ribs and wrenched limbs on our side. This was different. Temporary peace for the coronation, all sweetness and light and a chance to show what pleasant and reasonable people we were, in spite of little problems like not having the vote.

The messenger left. Jessie started on her question to me again and this time, to my regret, managed to complete it.

'Nell, have you bought your white dress yet? Mrs Swan says you're being difficult.'

Mrs Swan was the marshal for the section of the parade that was supposed to include me.

'I wouldn't call it difficult. It's just with seven hundred prisoners, I shouldn't have thought I'd be missed.'

Jessie gave me a look.

'Nell, your place is with the rest of the prisoners. Please don't . . .'

'Make trouble?'

'Exactly. Dickins and Jones are doing a very nice line in white cotton dresses specially for the procession at twenty-seven shillings and sixpence. If you get along there first thing tomorrow as soon as they open I'm sure they'll find something to fit you, even with your height.'

I hate wearing white. My delight in pageantry is limited. The idea of marching through the streets of London dressed as for a garden party, behind Joan of Arc on a white horse, was not my idea of a profitable way to spend Saturday evening. But it seemed there was no escape. The head of the great procession was to be made up of women like myself who had served terms in prison for the cause, and it was clear that refusal to take part would be regarded as desertion. I sighed, thinking of all the things I'd rather do with twenty-seven shillings and sixpence, or thirty-five if you included a new, white straw hat. I'd returned gloomily to my work of writing a welcome for the French and Belgian delegates when salvation of a kind arrived in the form of another messenger.

'Nell, Mrs Pankhurst says will you please go and see her at once.'

As I went along the corridor to her room, dodging various flying figures along the way, I hoped that I wasn't heading for another argument. I admire our leader Emmeline as much as anybody, but there's no denying the fact that I'm not her favourite person. She knows very well that I've been useful from time to time to the movement in ways that can't always be made public, but she has doubts about my methods. Frequently I have doubts about my methods as well, but there's not always much choice. I was beginning to notice that my friends and associates tended to fling me into awkward situations, then raise eyebrows about the steps I had to take to get out of them.

There were two people in the room, Emmeline seated at her desk, crowded with papers and telegrams and, striding around the room, the short stocky figure of Flora Drummond, known by one and all as 'The General'. She'd been talking as I came in and broke off to say, 'There you are at last, Nell,' as if they'd been waiting all day. She looked harassed, as well she might, being the one in charge of the parade. Emmeline was more stately and invited me to sit down.

'The General's just raised something with me, Nell. I thought you might be the person to advise us.'

3

The General came to a halt in front of me.

'The point is, we don't want trouble tomorrow.'

I decided not to say anything. She waited, then went on.

'We've been getting a few disturbing reports that some people might be out to make it. Not from our side, of course.'

'The anti-suffragists?'

They both nodded. There were, we knew, several societies of varying degrees of eccentricity campaigning against giving women the vote. Although they attracted the predictable complement of batty clergymen and elderly peers who still hadn't recovered from the shock of the Magna Carta, the odd thing was that most of them were headed by women. Their line was that while women were free to get everything they wanted by marrying rich men and using domestic blackmail to control them, it was unfeminine to soil their gloves with dirty things like politics.

'Can they really cause us much trouble? They may shout a bit, I suppose, but nobody will hear them over all our bands.' (At last count, we had at least sixty of those lined up, including Scottish pipers.)

Emmeline said, 'Suppose it were worse than that?'

'Have we any reason for thinking it will be?'

'We've been hearing a few things, haven't we, Flora?'

She sounded serious. I knew that between them they ran a good intelligence network and we had sympathisers in some unexpected places.

'They're not usually very effective.'

'They don't need to do much. Any disturbance, however minor, will be twisted by our opponents to look like our fault. The whole of London will be watching our parade tomorrow. It must go without the slightest flaw.'

The General listened and nodded.

'That's where we thought you could help, Nell. If we might regard you as a kind of roving steward, keeping your eyes open for anything out of the way and nipping it in the bud, I'm sure we could feel a great deal more confident.'

With a procession five miles long that was a tall order. On the other hand, I didn't rate the possible opposition highly.

'I'd need a few helpers.'

'Anybody you want,' said Emmeline generously. She added at once, 'Only don't take too many out of the procession, will you?'

'A dozen should do it. And we'd better not wear white. It will be easier if we can mingle with the crowds.'

I got a couple of nods to that, and permission to recruit whoever I needed, on the General's authority. As I walked back along the corridor my chief feeling was relief that I shouldn't have to walk in step and waste thirty-five shillings.

A mistake, of course.

TWO

SATURDAY WAS A FINE DAY, sunshine and only a few clouds in a blue sky. The roads along the Embankment were full of people strolling, waiting without knowing quite what they were waiting for with the coronation itself still six days away, but good humoured. The air quivered with the sounds of hammering and planks thumping down off lorries and wagons as teams of workmen put up the stands along the route from Buckingham Palace to Westminster Abbey. At some time during the morning Their Majesties arrived by train from Windsor Castle and drove from Paddington to the palace. I heard the distant cheering as I and my hastily recruited team of watchwomen went round the route our parade would take in the evening, trying to guess where the dreaded trouble might raise its head.

It was, if you took it too seriously, an impossible brief I'd been given. The main procession would be forming up in two streams along the entire length of the Embankment, from Blackfriars Bridge in the East all the way to Westminster Bridge alongside the Houses of Parliament. The two streams would converge at the bottom of Northumberland Avenue and flow along Pall Mall and Piccadilly through Knightsbridge to Kensington and the Albert Hall. Keeping a constant check on this route would have over-taxed an army. I'd worked out the night before that if our anti-vote opponents really were planning disruption, they'd choose a place where the impact would be greatest and the crowds thickest, probably between Pall

6

Mall and Hyde Park Corner. I planned to station a few scouts along this area, with runners operating between them, to watch for any groups behaving suspiciously.

'If you do see anything,' I told them, 'for goodness' sake don't try and deal with it yourself. Your job is to find the nearest police officer, tell him about it as clearly and factually as you can, then get word to me. Remember, today the police are on our side.'

I got some odd looks when I said that, and I could feel my collar-bone twitching. It had been broken when I was sat on by two constables outside the House of Commons last November. Several of my team had similar memories and were unconvinced. But our leaders had been co-operating closely with the police in planning this evening's entirely legal and peaceful demonstration and Emmeline's final instruction to me, emphatically delivered, was that this truce was on no account to be upset, no matter what happened.

All these preparations took a fair part of the morning, then I had to take some of the afternoon off to play my part in welcoming supporters who'd come from other parts of Europe to march with us. By the time this was over it was four o'clock and the ranks were already beginning to form up in the broad road alongside the Thames. In spite of my scepticism about pageantry I felt a tightness in the chest as I stood in the sunshine on Blackfriars Bridge and looked up the river towards the pinnacles of Westminster. Running parallel to the Thames all the way was another river almost as wide made up entirely of humanity, mostly women, with a gentle humming sound of tens of thousands of voices rising from it. Our colours of white, purple and green predominated, but there were pink wreaths of roses around the float representing the Empire, the blue and silver banner of the Artists' Suffrage League, black, white and gold for the writers, blue and white for the Catholic Women's Suffrage Society, the red of the Fabian Women. The Musicians' Contingent, under the formidable charge of Dr Ethel Smyth, were already tuning up and practising the new marching song she'd composed for us:

'Shout, shout up with your song,
Cry with the wind for the dawn is breaking.
March, march swing you along,
Wide blows our banner and hope is waking.'

Everyone on the march had been supplied with copies of the words and ordered to learn them by heart.

As we got near the starting time of half-past five I decided to move up towards the front of the march, in case any opposition was planned at that point. The leaders were ready and waiting, Joan of Arc on her white horse, General Drummond, also on horseback in dark green riding habit, the New Crusaders with their banners, Emmeline in white with flowers on her bodice and a cockade of purple, white and green feathers in her hat, Christabel in her academic gown. Then, formed up behind their banner 'From Prison to Citizenship', the seven hundred women who'd served their time. Dozens of these were friends of mine and called out greetings as I went past, along with a few cheerful insults because I wasn't marching with them. There were others whose faces I could remember, but not always names, women young enough to be within a few years of their schooldays, old enough to be grand-mothers, daughters of aristocratic families or Lancashire mill workers, all with this one thing in common.

''ello, Nell.'

A cheerful greeting in a Cockney voice from a woman in her twenties at the end of a line. A small, eager face with a jutting chin and bright eyes looking out from a mass of dark brown crinkly hair. I remembered the face but struggled to put a name to it. She laughed.

'Remember 'olloway? DX4?'

Her cell number, three doors up from mine. The name came to me.

8

'Violet. Violet White. Well, I didn't expect to see you here.'

The bright eyes turned wary and watchful, the cheerful voice a shade combative.

'Why not? Why shouldn't I be?'

'Well, it's just . . .'

Eyes were turning towards us. Don't make trouble, I reminded myself.

'I've been in prison like the rest of them, haven't I? I've got a right to be here.'

The first statement was quite true, the second debatable. Violet White had indeed served time in prison, but not for the cause. She was in Holloway for the same offence as a lot of the young women there: persistent soliciting. She'd been caught by the police in Covent Garden once too often and had been sent down for three months. I looked at her bright eyes, the tilt of her chin and registered that eyes were turning towards us.

'You've got a perfect right to march, of course. In fact you're welcome. But there are other sections in the procession where you might . . .'

I was playing for time, trying to find inspiration. Her gaze didn't waver.

'Like where?'

A good question. I remembered that there was a section amongst the professional groups called 'sweated women', representing the over-worked and underpaid, mostly made up of garment trade workers from the East End.

'What are you grinning at?'

'Err . . . nothing.'

I glanced at her dress of virginal white muslin, her jaunty little hat with pink roses. Not sweated women.

'I asked the woman on the horse where the prisoners were and she sent me here. Are you telling me I've got no right to be here?'

I looked at the little hat, the bright eyes and thought of Holloway.

9

'No, Violet. I'm not telling you that. Good luck and enjoy the march.'

I left her to it. As I turned back to wave to her she was happily chatting to the rest of the women, who'd naturally assume that she was a suffragette they hadn't happened to meet before. I walked away, still grinning to myself. I was happily convinced in my own mind that to have extracted Violet from the ranks of the prison martyrs would have been a blemish on the occasion, not to speak of being embarrassing and difficult to do since she seemed determined about it. On the other hand, I was equally sure that Emmeline wouldn't like it. If our leader ever found out that I'd allowed a known and convicted prostitute to march under false colours near the head of our great procession, all of my past sins would pale in comparison. Still, there was no reason that she ever would find out. When the bands began playing and the prisoners moved off behind their banner, there was Violet with the rest.

'March, march – many as one
Shoulder to shoulder and friend to friend.'

It was a good song, though by eight o'clock that evening, with the tail end of the great procession still passing along Piccadilly, I thought I shouldn't care if I didn't hear it again for a month or two. All through the evening it had surged above the columns of marchers, between the solid faces of the gentlemen's clubs of Pall Mall, past the cliffs of the rich houses in Knightsbridge. But in spite of sore feet and an aching head from not having time to stop for food all day, I was relieved and light hearted at how well it had all gone. The crowd had loved it. It was a new experience for us to be cheered by the public, but cheered we'd been. Never mind whether most of the people who cheered believed in our cause or not. Some of them almost certainly didn't. The point was we were giving them a pre-coronation spectacle on a scale that had never been seen before and they liked the colour and energy of it.

My job had been easy. Very little trouble from start to finish. True, the anti-suffragists had hired sandwichmen to trot round with placards stating 'Women do NOT want the vote', but they'd only contributed to the general amusement. An outbreak of a few urchins throwing stones at Hyde Park Corner had been smartly dealt with by myself and a couple of assistants without needing to involve the police. As I went up and down the procession route I occasionally found myself face to face with police constables on much the same errand as my own and, amazingly, a kind of temporary alliance developed.

'Evening, Miss Bray. Having a good time, are we?'

This, from a solid officer I'd last met when he was arresting me in Downing Street. He smiled, I smiled, we went on our separate beats and I wondered if the next pigeon I saw would be flying upside down.

At eight o'clock I was on my last patrol, standing down the watchwomen so that they could go and at least catch the tail end of the rally in the Albert Hall. Once all the messages had been delivered I decided to walk back to where the very last contingents of the procession would be forming up near Westminster Bridge. It would be almost dark before they'd finished marching but the enthusiasm was undimmed. The waiting sections were filling the road between the river and the white stone and redbrick premises of Scotland Yard. There were even a few policemen hanging out of open windows looking down at them, but without hostility. These last sections included the cohorts of our male supporters, like the Men's League for Women's Suffrage and various other friends and sympathisers. There was one group made up of men from the universities in academic gowns and mortar boards. Among them I recognised an old friend.

'Simon Frater. Nice of you to be here.'

Simon is a lecturer in ancient history and philosophy at London University. He stood out from the crowd as he always did, more than six feet tall and as thin as a column

in a ledger, always looking slightly baffled to find himself wherever he happened to be, as if he'd started the day in ancient Athens then found himself by some inexplicable accident elsewhere in time and place. When it came to writing or debating, he had one of the most lucid minds I'd ever encountered, but his life, and the lives of his friends, were complicated by his almost uncanny ability to attract disaster. If a branch of a tree happened to fall in any of the home counties, Simon would be standing beneath it. Mechanical things came apart in his hands and lecture notes scattered to the four winds like leaves. Small dogs, comatose for years, would rise up and sink their teeth into him. And yet he was the kindest and mildest of men, reacting to all these disasters without annoyance, only a kind of stoic puzzlement. His nature and sense of humour brought him friends by the dozen, which was just as well because he needed every one of them to steer him along the precipice between one drama and the next.

To add to his problems he had a keen sense of justice and chivalry, which was what had brought him into the Votes for Women struggle. The sense of justice was welcome, but the chivalry caused us problems. For instance, in last November's fracas outside Parliament he'd sailed in to try to rescue a woman who was being battered by two large policemen. It was brave, but unwise given that his fighting skills were non-existent. When the two policemen turned on him I'd had to go to his rescue, which is how my collar-bone came to be broken. Not his fault. The problem was that his mind moved far too fast for his body to keep up with it. This meant that he was in a continuous state of self-contradictory motion. It was as if his brain were playing some wild music all the time and his body could never learn to dance to it, try as it would.

He saw me, shouted 'Nell', and stepped on the toe of the man behind him, backing into the one in front as he turned to make his apologies. He managed to extricate himself and joined me on the pavement. We talked about the success of the procession.

'I really do congratulate you all. Nobody can argue now that women are incapable of organisation. And just look at the public support.'

A wide sweep of his arm took in a motley crowd stretching right back across Westminster Bridge. There were hundreds of pedestrians not officially part of the march, probably the kind who'll join anything that moves, and a collection of private motor cars and horse-drawn carriages waiting more or less patiently. Among them one strange vehicle stood out.

It was at our end of the bridge, so that when the procession began to move a few steps would carry it round the corner and onto the Embankment opposite Scotland Yard. Flat and decrepit, it looked as if it might be taking the evening off from being a milk float, drawn by a raw-boned bay cob that was leaning against the collar of its harness, head down, more than half asleep. It was a heavy load for one cob to pull because there were six people on it, including the driver, all of them in elaborate fancy dress with huge masks completely covering their heads. There was a ragged lion, a silvery thing that might quite possibly have been intended for a unicorn, a knight in cardboard armour carrying a shield with GOD HELP THE KING painted on it and, sitting on a dais draped in red, white and blue, a creature with a huge white head like Humpty Dumpty with a golden crown on top. It wore a wig of tangled string and a loose white robe that billowed out in the breeze from the river. Behind it stood a man in white shirt and black trousers holding an enormous axe. His head and shoulders were covered with a black hood with slits for eyes. An executioner. Simon stared at it, took off his glasses and gave them a polish, stared again.

'Ye gods, is that one of yours?'

'Certainly not.'

There were very few floats in our official procession and all those would be well into Kensington by now. Besides, even from where we were standing there was something unmistakably louche and tatty about this ensemble, a

13

long way from the carefully crafted objects in the women's procession.

Simon said tolerantly, 'Oh well, as long as they're on the right side . . .'

'You know, I'm not so sure about that.'

The longer I looked at it, the more suspicious I got. The spectators wouldn't know that this thing was not one of ours and if some jokers, or some of our political opponents, took a ride on the tail of our procession apparently holding king and country up to ridicule, a lot of the good effect of the day would be undone.

'I'm going for a look at that thing,' I said. 'You stay here.'

THREE

I WALKED QUICKLY TOWARDS THE traffic on the bridge, but just as I started it began to move forward, onto the Embankment. A carriage of spectators at the head of the line drew smoothly away, but the bay cob pulling the float seemed to have gone to sleep entirely. There were cries of 'Wake up, England' from the traffic on the bridge behind them, some tooting of motor car horns. There seemed to be signs of perturbation among the tableau. The royal figure was getting up, its movements accentuated by the swaying of the gross papier mâché head. The lion was waving its paws around and the driver on the box was flapping the reins at the horse and cursing it. He cursed in a language I couldn't identify, though the meaning was obvious, and tried to give it a cut with his whip but it takes practice to manage a whip and he was clearly no coachman. The lash curled out half-heartedly, flicked the shoulder of a spectator. The friendly bantering from the crowd turned to murmurs of indignation. The cob woke up and lurched forward, jolting the group on the cart. The royal figure was doing an ungainly kind of jig, the head still smirking above it like a great balloon. The executioner was joining in, scuffling wildly. They were thrown against each other by the movement of the cart and appeared to be wrestling. Then I heard a familiar voice at my shoulder.

'You're right, Nell, they're not one of yours.'

Simon, close behind me although I told him to stay where he was. But before I had time to be annoyed about that there was a shout from the crowd.

15

'They're on fire.'

There was a whiff of burning fabric in the air. The draperies around the king's podium were smouldering. The executioner, still impassively hooded, was trying to stamp them out with his anachronistic brown leather boots while the lion, the unicorn and the knight drew back towards the edge of the cart. The unchanging expressions of their masks while their bodies registered fear and unease were part of the dreamlike quality of what was happening. The rest of the crowd took up the shout, calling for water, yelling to the figures on the cart to jump. Their noise galvanised the old cob and it followed the respectable carriage ahead of it at a shambling trot, heading for the Embankment and the rest of the procession. The driver dropped the reins and seemed to be contemplating jumping off.

A satirical float, on fire and driverless, spoiling the end of our beautiful procession, was exactly the kind of incident I was supposed to prevent. I ran along beside it, stumbling from pavement to gutter, pushing through the crowd, with the idea that if the driver did abandon the box I would have to clamber aboard and somehow bring the equipage to a halt. I didn't have time to see what Simon was doing and hoped he'd keep out of trouble. Just as we were about to turn onto the Embankment the carriage in front came to a sudden halt and the cob stopped as abruptly as he'd started. I looked over the heads of the crowd and saw a sprinkling of blue uniforms ahead. Somebody at Scotland Yard must have seen what was going on and the police were coming. About time too, I thought, glad to pass on the responsibility.

At that point, three things happened so close together that I remember them as simultaneous. One was that the driver seized the opportunity to clamber off the box and run away, jabbing at the crowd with his whip so that they gave way, protesting. Another was the shot. It came, without a shadow of a doubt, from the back of the cart. When it happened I was watching the driver running away.

16

By the time I turned to look at the cart the tatty lion had clambered from the back of it onto the box and seized the reins, with a roughness and decision that jerked the cob's head up and his jaw open. The lion hauled the horse's head round and the animal, scared by the noise of the shot and the crowd, plunged crossways across the end of the bridge, scattering people in all directions, then turned round so that it was facing the opposite bank. With the lion wielding the whip and shouting in a harsh but female voice it went away at a crazy canter, swerving past cars and carriages. The executioner was still stamping out the fire, managing somehow to keep his feet. The knight fell to his knees and pulled the unicorn down with him. He seemed to be trying to prevent it from jumping off the cart, a crazy idea at that speed. His helmet had fallen off or perhaps he'd thrown it off. I had a sideview of a bulging forehead, wispy beard and hair flying in the breeze.

The king figure had fallen sideways, the huge head rolling with the motion of the cart like a discarded eggshell on a windy beach. Something black was crouching beside it, a bereaved bird, angular and flapping. It took me a full second to realise that the flapping thing was Simon, his academic gown blowing out from the speed and his own agitation. He'd taken hold of the king's head and from where I was standing it looked as if he was trying to wrench it away from the body. While I'd been watching the driver running away he must somehow have managed to clamber onto the cart, decisively disastrous as ever. I ran across the bridge after them, aware of shouting and footsteps pounding behind me. They reached the south side of the bridge and, still cantering, took a right hand swerve towards Lambeth, flinging bird and egg and the body still attached to egg onto the road. They lay there in a huddle and when I got to them Simon was still getting to his knees, staring down at the thing beside him.

'Nell . . .' He looked up at me, dazed. 'I . . . I think he's dead, Nell.'

He put his hand up to adjust his glasses, leaving a long

smear of red down his white cheek. A pulse in his neck was twitching. He could hardly speak. Under the gown, his white shirt was soaked red.

'I was trying . . . trying to lift him up and I found . . .'

His other hand had been concealed in the fold of his gown. Now he held it out to me, showing the thing he was holding.

'It's a gun, Nell.'

Almost as if he doubted it.

'Yes. Was it lying beside him?'

He nodded and got to his feet unsteadily. The man in the king's head was dead beyond·a doubt. Nothing live could lie so limply, or have leaked such a puddle of blood. From the chest, I thought. He was lying sideways on the road, just as he'd fallen.

'I think you'd better let me have it.'

I doubted if he'd ever handled a gun in his life before. It was a revolver, shaking in his hand so that it pointed at nothing or everything. The pounding feet had almost reached us.

'Put that gun down.'

A hoarse, breathless shout from a police constable, red and sweating. There were more behind him.

'Put it down.'

To say that Simon fired a shot would imply a control over his movements that he certainly didn't have by that point. Indisputably, the gun fired because the noise and the powder reek were all round us, blotting out thought for an instant. The bullet must have gone somewhere, probably over the bridge parapet and into the river, certainly nowhere near any of us. There was gaping surprise on the face of the police officer, consternation on Simon's. He still had a grip on the revolver and now turned it upright, looking into the barrel to see how the trick was worked.

'What made it go . . .?'

I shouted to him to drop it, but it was the police constable who probably saved him from putting a bullet through his own brain in a spirit of mazed experiment.

18

'I'll take that, if you please, sir.'

Simon handed it over as simply as a borrowed pencil. He was still staring at me, waiting for me to make sense of things, when a whole huddle of police surrounded him, two attaching themselves to each arm, holding him penned between them. In a puzzled way, he tried to shake them off. They twisted his arms behind him. He winced and the pulse in his neck throbbed faster.

'Simon, don't do anything.'

'But why . . .'

A police sergeant arrived. The first constable showed him the revolver and said Simon had tried to shoot him.

'Of course he didn't. He'd just picked up the gun and it went off. Have you got people following that cart? It could be anywhere in Lambeth by now.'

The knot of constables looked at the sergeant. He was hot and annoyed with himself, for having to run or not running fast enough, and gripped by the need to take decisive action that so often leads to disaster, especially among people in uniform.

'Are you with this man?'

'Yes, but don't worry about that now. It was somebody on that cart who shot him. It will be . . .'

I tried to move out from the crowd of police, to see if the cart was still in view. The sergeant seemed to think I was trying to escape and grabbed me by the arm, not particularly hard as these things go, but more than enough to wake Simon's unwanted chivalry.

'Officer, unhand that woman.'

Constabular jaws dropped all round him. Sheer surprise loosened their grip enough for Simon to pull himself away and move towards me and the sergeant. Shouting at him and each other, they closed on him again and he disappeared under a scrum of dark blue. I tried to tell him not to resist, but it did no good. By the time they'd pulled him upright again he was in no shape to resist anyway. The sergeant gave an order and he was hustled, glasses hanging from one ear and footsteps dragging, back to the Scotland Yard side of the bridge.

A crowd parted to let them through. It was being kept back by a line of policemen. Two more constables were preventing traffic and passengers entering from the south side, which left me and the surrounding police on our own on the wide expanse of bridge, apart from the body. Two of them were kneeling beside it by now but it was clear from the lack of urgency about them that there was nothing to be done. They had at least removed the mockery king's head. It was standing there in the road, smiling its inane smile, gold paper crown on top of a wig of old rope teased out into yellow ringlets. Clever piece of work in its way. The man who'd worn it was turned onto his back. Close to, his royal robe was a yellowed flannel nightdress soaked with blood, the bright wetness spreading from the chest and down the folds. At one end battered boots stuck out, at the other a young rounded face with a dark beard, eyes staring.

The sergeant said, 'Cover him up, for God's sake.'

There was a blue sheet in the road that had been part of the patriotic draperies fallen or thrown off the cart, scorched round the edges, and they spread it over the body. A linen sheet, good quality once with some sort of bird and pomegranate design and linked letters in a monogram woven into it in glossier thread, showing through the streaks of royal blue dye. Funny the things you notice.

The sergeant turned his attention back to me. I sensed he was at a loss and knew how he felt. He'd been there to police a peaceful procession and now he had this on his hands. As factually as I could I told him about seeing the cart and the fire.

'And this friend of yours with the gun was on the cart, was he?'

'He wasn't on the cart to start with. I think he only got up there to help them put out the fire. And he didn't have a gun. He must have picked it up from beside the body.'

20

His expression showed total scepticism. I felt the beginnings of panic at how bad things looked for Simon, tried to stay calm.

'What's his name, this friend of yours?'

'Frater. Simon Frater. But he had nothing to do with it. This man was shot by somebody on the cart with him. They're all in fancy dress. If you're lucky you might still catch them before they've got time to change.'

I restrained myself from adding that even the Metropolitan Police should be capable of spotting a lion and a unicorn in Lambeth. His hand was still clamped on my arm and it was all I could do not to chase off after them, dragging him with me. He didn't move.

'It was your friend who shot at us.'

'Of course he didn't. Simon's no more capable of trying to shoot somebody than flying.'

Unfriendly laughter from some of the constables. The sergeant's voice became more formal.

'I must ask you to accompany me back to Scotland Yard.'

'I'll accompany you anywhere you like, but for goodness' sake send some of your men after that cart.'

He must have felt my unwillingness to move, insupportable in front of the constables still indignant from being under fire.

'You're under arrest.'

Two more constables closed in on me.

'What in the world for?'

'Obstructing the police in the course of their duty.'

Useless to protest. Obstruction can mean practically anything the police want it to mean. They escorted me across the bridge, through the police cordon and the crowd uncertain whether to cheer or jeer. The street in front of Scotland Yard was still full of the final instalment of our march waiting to move off, buzzing and fidgety to know what had been happening on the bridge. A closed motor vehicle was nosing its way through with a worried constable at the wheel.

21

'Be going to pick up the body,' said one of my escorts. The sergeant, nervy and unhappy, told him to be quiet. We went up the steps and into Scotland Yard.

As the door closed behind us I heard a band starting up raggedly again from the street, voices singing:

'March, march, swing you along.
Wide blows our banner and hope is waking.'

The march was on its way again. I hoped nobody would tell Emmeline until later. Much later.

FOUR

AT FIRST THEY PUT ME in an ordinary room, not a cell. I was questioned by a succession of police, first an inspector with the sergeant who'd arrested me in attendance, then two men in plain clothes. I could only tell them over again the story exactly as it happened. No, I hadn't ever before seen the young man who'd been shot. No, I'd known nothing in advance about the cart, and it had only been the merest of hunches that it might cause trouble. I suggested that they should get in touch with the offices of the Women's Social and Political Union in Clement's Inn to check my story that I was acting as a march steward. I'd thought about this and only suggested it with reluctance, but I had to involve the movement to that extent or our stories would have looked even less likely. They kept coming back to Simon. I tried hard to make them realise how unaggressive he was, how impossible it was that he should shoot anybody, but felt increasingly despairing of getting them to understand. By their account he'd deliberately fired at a group of policemen and was capable of anything. I knew that they'd be questioning him somewhere in the same building, probably more harshly than this, and hoped without much optimism that he was keeping his head. Even at best of times he was easily depressed and this was probably the worst thing that had ever happened to him.

The two in plain clothes were more aggressive than the uniformed police. A thin man with sunken eyes and black eyebrows did most of the questioning, but I had the impression that the man beside him was the one to watch. He was probably still in his twenties but had the air of already advancing confidently on middle age. It came from his broad fleshy chin, the narrow eyes that turned down at the outside corners, deep downward lines from his snout-like nose to his mouth, an expression both self-satisfied and wary. It was the look you see sometimes on plump elderly labradors that would bite you if they could summon up the energy. The thin man called him Mr Brust, and seemed anxious for his good opinion, though Brust was the younger of the two.

The process of questioning made my entirely rational actions seem like eccentricity. Brust in particular looked sceptical when I said I was worried the driver might abandon his post and that I'd have to take over the reins.

'What did you propose to do then, Miss Bray?'

'Hand it over to a policeman, I suppose. I'd no intention of keeping it, I promise you.'

I hoped that a charge of attempted kidnap was not to be included among my sins and decided I should be allowed some questions.

'The sergeant said he was arresting me for obstructing the police but I haven't been formally charged yet. Am I still accused of obstruction?'

I'd been charged with obstructing the police once before, but there hadn't been this elaboration about it and I'd been in front of a magistrate within two hours on that occasion. The thin man glanced at Brust, who spoke reluctantly.

'We are investigating a murder.'

'Yes, so why this nonsense about obstructing the police? If you really think that Mr Frater and I were involved in some kind of plot, which is the most ridiculous thing I've heard in my life, why aren't you charging me with that?'

'That's for us to decide.'

'Have you caught up with the cart yet?'

Another glance from the thin man to the younger man, but this time he got no help and had to manage on his own.

24

'A search is proceeding.'

Which meant they hadn't. Surely the characters would abandon the cart and costumes as soon as they got into a quiet street on the other side of the river.

'If you hadn't wasted time arresting us, you'd have caught up with them.'

Brust decided to go back to the old subject.

'Mr Frater is a friend of yours?'

'A friend and colleague for several years.'

'Colleague?'

'In the suffragette movement. He helps to organise one of our supporting groups among the university men.'

The downward creases on Mr Brust's face grew even deeper. He disapproved.

'A professor, is he?'

'Not yet. He's a lecturer, but very distinguished. He's just published a book on Roman politics. *The Times* reviewed it very well last week.'

I thought they should know that Simon was a respectable citizen. Soon after that the two plain-clothes men stood up to leave. I asked to speak to a lawyer.

All in good time, they said. The door closed.

Later that evening I was formally charged with obstructing the police, then transferred in a closed carriage across a mile of London to the cells at Bow Street police station to await an appearance in front of the magistrates. There was no sign of Simon and I knew it would be useless to ask about him. When you're a prisoner the mental landscape changes. The simplest and most natural things – having a drink of water, going to the lavatory, asking a question and getting an answer – become a matter of negotiation and permission, of knowing whom to ask, when to ask and, more often, when not to ask. As soon as the first door had closed on me at Scotland Yard it had all come washing back over me and it was even stronger at Bow Street because I'd spent other nights in the police cells there while awaiting trial and it was all familiar.

There was the same smell of disinfectant hanging over everything, the same hollow echo of the warders' and wardresses' feet along the corridor, sounds of doors opening and slamming, muffled sobbing, a drunken voice, shushed by the warders and raised again minutes later, '. . . 'twas there sweet Annie Laurie gave me her promise true'. Last time I was in it had been 'Danny Boy'. The perfectly civil wardress who locked me in told me I'd have a cell to myself at first, but I'd probably have to double up before the night was out. It was an unusually busy Saturday, she said, on account of the coronation. After the whirling events of the past few hours it felt almost reassuringly familiar, but as I settled on the wooden bench against the wall that was the cell's only furniture I knew I couldn't, for Simon's sake, let myself relax back into that familiarity. Last time it had all been simple enough. I'd been guilty as charged of various offences against public order for the cause, along with others. It had been just a matter of appearing in court and going to prison and that was that. This time I was on my own. Worse than on my own. I'd dragged somebody else into serious trouble and from where I was sitting I could think of no way to do anything about it.

I never for a moment took seriously the idea that Simon might have shot the man in the king's head. I was sure that he, like me, had known nothing about the cart. It was inconceivable that he'd own or carry a gun. Apart from anything else, to climb onto the cart and shoot a man in the few seconds available would have meant moving with a speed and effectiveness quite alien to his nature. Even after the accident with the gun I'd assumed that it was only a matter of time and explanation before the police saw how harmless he was. It was the interview with the two plain-clothes men, especially the younger one, that began to convince me otherwise. Something odd was going on, something so odd that the murder charge had to be taken seriously. I'd been so occupied with telling my story of events, and willing the police to believe me, that the questions of what the party on the float were doing and how the man came to be killed had been pushed to the back of my mind. Sitting there, feeling deathly tired and more than a little hungry, I tried to drag them to the front of it.

I'd been right at least in thinking there was something sinister about the cart. It wasn't one of ours. The driver, when annoyed, was swearing in a language I didn't recognise, which was peculiar in itself as I could identify all the main European languages, including Russian. It had a guttural, northern quality to it rather than a southern rhythm. Finnish, Latvian, Estonian? I had a hunch that was the area. The only face I'd seen, apart from the driver's, belonged to the knight in cardboard armour and he could have been almost any nationality. I'd given the police a description of him, such as it was, but it would have fitted several hundred men in London. There was something else at the back of my mind, something that I hadn't told the police because it hadn't occurred to me.

'. . . and for bonnie Annie Laurie I would lie me down and . . .'

'Shut up in there, number five, or *I'll* bloody well come in and lie you down.'

Hard to concentrate in here. Something about the blue-dyed sheet, good quality linen. Soon after that, supper came round, a mug of greyish cocoa and a beef sandwich, dry and curly as the brim of a bowler hat. I stretched out on the bench and tried to sleep but was woken in the early hours by the tired wardress with a cell mate for me, a little grey-haired woman with mad eyes and a monotonous vocabulary. I gave her the bench and took to the floor and she muttered throughout the night about enemies in high places and how the Archbishop of Canterbury was plotting to kill her. I hoped Simon was sleeping better.

In the morning, I had a visitor. It was a clamorous morning because although it was a Sunday the Bow Street magistrates were sitting to deal with the Saturday night harvest of drunks, prostitutes and miscellaneous unfortunates. Keys rattled, our cell door was flung open and Catherine came in, hands stretched out.

'Oh Nell, what have you gone and done this time?'

Catherine's a music teacher, one of my friends in the movement, warm-hearted but inclined to take a dramatic view of things. Obviously some news had got through to Clement's Inn. Before I could reply she produced sandwiches from the bulging leather music case she always carried, being wise in the ways of prison visiting. People on remand in police cells are allowed to have food brought in by friends.

'I've got soap and a comb in here too. You never have one with you. And some pencils and writing paper.'

A brown wrinkled hand shot out from the bench behind us, grabbed one of the sandwiches. Until then I'd assumed my cell mate was asleep. Catherine blinked, carried on.

'We didn't hear until nearly midnight last night. Of course we were all at the Albert Hall rally. A few of us went back to the office to tidy up, and there was this man from Scotland Yard.'

'Fat with a turned-down face?'

'No, thin and twitchy. Anyway, he told us you were under arrest and asked if it was true you were working as a steward on the march. Of course we knew it was no use trying to get in to see you till morning. Poor Jessie was quite frantic.'

'Has anybody told Emmeline yet?'

She nodded and bit her lip.

'I suppose she blames me as usual.'

'Well, she does tend to. Nell, what exactly's happened? What on earth did Simon Frater think he was doing?'

'How much did the man from Scotland Yard tell you?'

'He said a man had been killed on the march and Simon Frater had been charged with murdering him, and you with obstructing the police when they arrested him. They wanted to know what we knew about Simon, was he a supporter of the cause, and so on. Well, of course we couldn't deny he was.'

'I should hope not. It was entirely my fault.'

'Nell!'

'Not murder, for goodness' sake, neither of us had seen the man before. Has Simon got a solicitor?'

'I don't know.'

'Well, would you find out, and if he hasn't, get him one.'

'We've arranged the usual one for you. He should be here soon.'

'Good. Surely nobody really thought Simon Frater had killed somebody? The man was shot. Can you imagine Simon knowing what to do with a gun?'

'No but . . .'

She glanced towards the old woman, now curled up on the bench and asleep again with crumbs round her mouth.

'You know, he was angry with what the police did to us on Black Friday. It did occur to us he might have been carrying a gun in case anything like it happened again, and of course he's so clumsy, it just might have gone off accidentally . . .'

'No. Nothing like that. It wasn't Simon. It was one of the people on the float but the police let him get away. Don't let anybody think it was Simon, even by accident.'

I was seriously worried now. If even Simon's friends thought he might have done it, what chance did he have with the police?

'What float?'

'Didn't the police tell you that?'

I gave her a brief description of the events leading to the killing and saw her eyes widen.

'But what were they doing?'

'Goodness knows, but somebody's got to find out, because I don't think the police will. From their point of view they've arrested a man and that's it.'

29

'But what on earth was Robert Withering doing in a king's head?'

'Who?'

'That was the man who was shot.'

'Any relation to . . . ?'

'Son.'

'Ye gods.'

Harold Withering was a cabinet minister, not the worst of them, but no better than most. He came, as I remembered, from a family that had made its money in shoe factories and then gone into public life. Liberal, meaning only marginally less hide-bound than the Conservatives, wealthy.

'No wonder the police are nervous. What in the world did he think he was doing?'

It supported my first idea that the people on the float had intended to make a mock of our procession. It was the sort of half-witted upper-class joke in which a cabinet minister's son would be involved. Perhaps they'd brought the gun along with them as part of the joke and it had gone fatally wrong. But how did all that fit in with a coachman speaking a Baltic language and the atmosphere of panic about them, even before the shot?

'How on earth did you hear this?'

'Somebody knows Withering's aunt. It's not in the papers yet. I suppose it will be on Monday.'

Cabinet minister's son shot by suffragette supporter outside Parliament. I wouldn't put it past them. Brust's labrador face came to mind on a tide of anger and urgency.

'We need to talk to somebody in Withering's circle and find out if he might do this sort of thing. I can think of a couple of people who might know, if I . . .'

I was on the point of reaching for my coat and hat, until it came to me where I was. In a cell at Bow Street, shortly to appear before magistrates on a charge which, with my record, would see me go down for a month at least. Not a good starting point.

'Damn.'

'You haven't eaten any of the sandwiches. You know what the food's like.'

I tried to impress on her that all this must be told to the solicitor acting for Simon, and the movement must get him the best available. She said she'd do what she could, but I could see she was still struggling to find a foothold, and I didn't blame her. Before we'd got far with it the wardress came back to say time was up and Catherine had to go.

'Don't worry, Nell. We'll do all we can.'

Not enough. It needed me.

I had a decision to make at once. I'd soon be up in front of the magistrate and the question was whether it would be any help to Simon to bring some of this out in court. It might not be any use in trying to defend myself against an obstruction charge, but that was a lost cause anyway. If a police officer tells a police court magistrate that you obstructed him in the course of his duty, the verdict's usually a foregone conclusion. I decided that the best thing to do would be to have a word with the solicitor the movement would send for me. According to regulations, I should have some time alone with him before we went into court.

When I decided this, I hadn't allowed for the hurry and confusion – not to mention the collective bad temper – of an extra police court sitting on a Sunday morning. The usual swift and cursory process through cases speeded up to a gallop. As we waited in the room below the court we watched prisoners coming down the steps from the dock with the stunned expression of people who've collided with justice and still haven't realised what hit them. Two or three of them hadn't had time to sober up from the episodes that had put them in dock in the first place, but they could take their time about it now – thirty days in most cases. My solicitor arrived, panting something about having to get a cab all the way from Finchley Road, just as the wardress was telling me to stand up because my case was the one after next.

'Morning, Miss Bray. Obstruction, is it? Are we pleading guilty or not guilty?'

'Not guilty, but that isn't the point. Have they told you how it happened?'

He shook his head.

'It was when they were arresting Simon Frater for murder. I tried to tell the sergeant they were making a mistake.'

'Sure it was no worse than that?'

'No, listen. I'm sure the police don't believe me about Simon. If we can get a few things out in open court . . .'

'Number twenty-seven. Twenty-seven get ready, please.'

My number on the list. The wardress began to edge me towards the door.

'Miss Bray, I really don't think it will help us to go into all that before the magistrate. I shall tell the court that you only said it in the heat of the moment, that you deeply regret . . .'

'I don't. What I want you to do is to give me an opportunity to tell the court . . .'

'Where's number twenty-seven?'

Before my solicitor even had a chance to take off his outdoor coat, I was in dock.

The result was as expected. I hadn't appeared before this particular magistrate before, but he seemed obsessed with the fear that I was going to make a political speech. Naturally we've all made political speeches from the dock on occasions, but I really didn't intend to do it this time. What mattered was to get a few facts before the public before the inevitable happened and I found myself on the way to Holloway. The police sergeant from the day before read out his account of what happened in a gabbling monotone. His statement, obviously well rehearsed, made no mention at all of a murder. The story was that he had been engaged in trying to arrest a suspect for an offence, and I had tried to prevent him. I pleaded not guilty. My solicitor asked the police officer several questions, but they were all the wrong kind from my point of view, trying to establish that I hadn't laid a hand on the sergeant. I wanted to shout at him that it wasn't the point.

The magistrate, although obviously reluctant about it, had to give me a chance to speak in my defence.

'Sir, all I was trying to do was to point out to the officer that the man he was about to arrest could not possibly have committed the murder . . .'

A quiver ran round the courtroom at the word 'murder'. This wasn't meant to be on the Sunday morning case list.

'We're not hearing a murder case, Miss Bray.'

'I simply intended to point out to the police that the real suspects were escaping. The only people who could have shot Mr Withering . . .'

'Silence. I will not have you talking about irrelevant cases. You are charged with obstructing this officer in the course of his duty and you have entered a plea of not guilty. Have you anything to say in relation to that charge?'

I went on trying, up to the point where he threatened me with contempt of court and my solicitor was developing a facial tic from his attempts to signal to me to be quiet. After that, there was nothing for it but to hear him pronounce sentence.

'I find the prisoner guilty as charged. Thirty days in the second division.'

As I waited with other women prisoners in a downstairs room for the Black Maria to take us to Holloway, I was struck by the irony that it was, in itself, a light sentence. I might have been facing two or three months instead of thirty days. If it had come in the ordinary course of events, like a march on Parliament, I should have been feeling quite cheerful about it. Admittedly, nobody would welcome thirty days in Holloway, but I'd be out well before the summer was over. In the present circumstances, though, thirty days might as well have been thirty months for the damage they'd do to any attempt to help Simon. If

33

the people who'd been on the float could be found, they must be followed while the trail was hot. They might be half-way to the other side of the world by the time I came out of prison.

There was, too, the sense of injustice. On past occasions I'd knowingly done something against the law, so going to prison was fair enough. This was different. The cursory unfairness of my own court appearance and sentence was just a small part of it. There was the much larger fact that the police had arrested an innocent man and seemed to be in no great hurry to find the guilty ones. And – although events had moved too quickly for me to have sorted things out in my mind – there was a nag of something even worse than that. It had been there from the start and got worse during my interview with the two plain-clothes men from Scotland Yard. If they thought I was involved with Simon, why hadn't they charged me as an accomplice? If they didn't, why had I been charged with anything at all? It occurred to me that an apparently light sentence, just enough to keep me out of the way until the dust settled, might be no coincidence.

The door from the corridor was thrown back and another prisoner escorted in. A Cockney voice upraised told the wardress she needn't bloody well shove. The woman who entered was dressed in summer-like white muslin smocked around the bodice, and a small hat with artificial roses pinned to her crinkly hair. From the brim of the hat another decoration dangled, a bent and bedraggled rosette in our suffragette colours of purple, green and white.

'I'm bloody well going in, aren't I? I haven't got any bloody choice.'

The door closed. She stared round at us challengingly, hands on her hips.

'What are you lot bloody well staring at? Haven't you ever seen a political prisoner before?'

She noticed me.

''ello, Nell. Shoulder to shoulder, eh?'

34

'Hello, Violet.'

She came over and sat on the bench beside me, shunting another woman aside with a thrust of her angular hip.

'What did they get you for then?'

'Obstruction.'

'Bloody liars.'

'And you?'

'The usual.'

'Soliciting?'

'Yes, but I bloody well wasn't. He asked me, I didn't have to ask him. There I was marching along with the others and he . . .'

'Marching? You mean, the police arrested you for soliciting while you were actually on the march?'

She wriggled a bit. The woman on her other side gave her a poisonous look.

'Well, I suppose I'd dropped out then. We were coming up Piccadilly when this gentleman I know calls out to me from the crowd. He catches my eye and makes a sign with his thumb towards the park. Well, I wasn't that pleased, but he's one of my regulars and business is business, so I thought I'd just nip off into the park with him for ten minutes and catch up with the rest of you later. Only the police go and arrest me before we even get as far as the park gates. I asked, "Can't a lady take a stroll in the park with a gentleman acquaintance?" But it didn't do any good and of course he didn't stand up for me – "never seen the lady before in my life, officer". But it wasn't soliciting. I wouldn't even have seen him if he hadn't called out to me.'

I closed my eyes and leaned back against the wall. I was hearing all too clearly in my mind what Emmeline would say if she knew not only that I'd allowed a known prostitute to join the ranks of prison martyrs, but that she'd stepped out of the ranks to do business in Piccadilly. If that did come to her attention – and I hoped most fervently that it wouldn't – then prison might turn out to be the safest place for me.

'Did you tell the magistrate?'

'Tried to. Wouldn't listen. Three bloody months.'

I glanced at her. Up to that point she'd been combative, almost jaunty, but on the last few words her voice trailed away into misery. Her sharp little chin was quivering and her fingers curled on the edge of the bench like a bird's claws.

'But I'm not going to do three months. Why should I?'

'No choice, have you?' said the woman on the other side, sneering.

'Oh yes I have.'

'Listen to her. Royal pardon from His Majesty, for services rendered?'

Violet didn't reply. Her whole body was tense with resentment and misery and I sensed fear there as well. Soon after that we were ordered out into the yard and the Black Maria backed up. A wardress called out our names in alphabetical order, surnames first. 'White, Violet', was at the end of the list.

The sneering woman sniggered.

'Some white violet.'

Violet said nothing, but she was standing next to me and I felt her trembling with anger.

'Take no notice,' I whispered. 'Not worth it.'

She nodded. A policeman opened the back door of the van. A narrow corridor up the middle of it, doors on either side into black boxes each with its own door, each just big enough for one person.

'That watch. They'll take it off you.'

Until Violet said that, I'd forgotten the watch pinned to my blouse. It had belonged to my Scottish grandmother and was too elaborate and valuable for everyday wear, gold set with small diamonds and garnets. My own more serviceable watch had broken just as I was getting ready to go out on the morning before and, knowing that timing was important that day, I'd had to pin this one on instead. Of course, I hadn't expected to end the day in prison. It would have to be handed in with all other personal trinkets and kept safe, with luck, until my release.

'Better give it to me.'

'They'll take it off you as well.'

'You see if they do.'

I unpinned it as unobtrusively as possible and dropped it into the hand already cupped against my skirt to receive it. I couldn't see the point, but if it consoled Violet at what was obviously a bad time for her, she was welcome to the loan of it.

The policeman stood at one side of the steps up to the Black Maria, a wardress on the other.

'Come on then ladies, let's be having you. Don't all rush at once.'

Violet glanced at me, then started talking very quickly, almost crying.

'Can't stand it again. Bad enough last time, nearly went mad in there. Can't stand another three months of it.'

What could I say? That three months wasn't long, that it would soon pass? Not true, and Violet knew it. All I could do was grab her tense little hand and hold it until it was our turn to file into the van. The doors slammed, the wheels rolled and the familiar journey began.

FIVE

RECEPTION INTO HOLLOWAY WAS BECOMING routine for me – personal details demanded by stone-faced wardress who never looked you in the eye, bawled out to older wardress standing by the door with pencil and notebook. Same chipped enamel bath with a line of scum round it that was becoming practically archaeological by now, same piles of stiff, patched underwear, green serge skirts and blouses and clumping shoes that the wardresses made some pretence of sorting through to find things that more or less fitted. As usual, my height caused problems. You'd have thought I'd arranged it just to annoy them. Violet White had been ahead of me in the queue and, since there'd been no outcry I assumed that she had managed to hide the watch and it was with her in her cell by now. If so I hoped it would be some comfort for her. The last sight I'd had of her she'd been white-faced and holding back tears with difficulty. The argument with a couple of the other women that had begun in the yard of the police station had been going on in fierce whispers until the wardresses told them to be quiet and it was clear that Violet wasn't going to make things easy for herself.

Nor was I. I'd never repined at prison before. On those previous occasions it had been my own fault that I was there, even part of the job to be there. But this time was different. The job was outside, and being shut up was preventing me from doing it. If I'd been at liberty, I'd have been following the few clues I knew about – the ones the police should have been following if it hadn't been for their stubbornness about Simon. But I wasn't at liberty. I was sitting on a plank bed wearing a green blouse and skirt several inches too short for me, a ridiculous check apron, a cloth badge with the cell number DX1 5 pinned to my chest, lace-up shoes broad enough for punts on my feet. A few feet away from me on one side was an iron-barred window with ribbed glass so thick that it sieved out most of the summer daylight, on the other a black-painted door with a spy-hole in it so that the wardresses could look in at any time. And there, apart from occasional outings to the chapel or the exercise yard, I was stuck for the next thirty days.

For those first few hours in the cell anger and impatience made me feel imprisoned in a way I'd never done in the past. I got up and stamped up and down, up and down, the sliding of my feet in the clumsy shoes reminding me with each step how I was subject to other people's wills. I kept looking at the emergency handle by the door that, if pulled, would set a gong clanging in the corridor outside and bring wardresses to see what the trouble was. It was there for use in dire emergencies, like serious illness, and there were penalties for its misuse. All the same, I was tempted to yank at it until wardresses came running from all sides, to yell that an innocent man was accused of murder and somebody must do something about it. Of course, all that would have done would be to extend my sentence.

After an hour or two of this I calmed down. The one thing I could do was think and for that, at any rate, I had plenty of time. If I could only tease out some more leads to follow, then perhaps I could communicate them to people outside. Not easy, with only one censored letter and one brief visit under the eye and ear of wardresses permitted per month, but I had to find a way. I tried to think back to where I'd been before the interruptions of court appearance and sentence. The driver's voice. Finnish, Estonian, Latvian. It was the last possibility that I clung to because Latvian pointed in a particular direction.

As everybody in London had cause to know, it pointed to anarchists. Earlier in that same year there'd been a battle between police, soldiers and a gang of Latvian anarchists at a place called Sidney Street in the East End. It started after the Latvians had killed three policemen in an attempted robbery and ended with the troops called out and the Home Secretary cheering them on. Most of the anarchists had died in the battle. The Latvians had come to Britain in the first place to get away from the Czar's secret police. Not all Latvians were anarchists and I'd met some who were as anxious for a quiet life as anybody. All the same, there might be a link.

Assume, since I had to start somewhere, that the driver of the float was Latvian. Take another jump, and assume he was an anarchist. It wasn't unthinkable that an anarchist group might want to lay on some sort of anti-Royalist demonstration in advance of the coronation. What had attracted my attention to the float in the first place had been a certain satirical air about it. It would have been a lot more effective to have done it during the coronation procession itself, but that would be so thick with police and soldiers that they wouldn't have stood a chance. Our own procession through the heart of London, highly publicised but less rigorously policed, might have seemed to them the next best thing. So far so good, but there was a problem: the identity of the victim Robert Withering. The presence of a cabinet minister's son fitted in much better with my earlier idea of some unfunny joke on us by the smug classes. In which case my Latvian – if indeed he were a Latvian – might be no more than some harmless political refugee taken on as Daddy's groom and co-opted for the occasion. There was another problem with that. Young Robert had been shot dead, almost certainly by one of his companions on the float. That hardly went with a public school practical joke.

I heard the tramp of feet along the corridor, keys rattling, doors being flung back. Why is it that nobody ever opens a door in a prison quietly? Even this early evening routine, letting the prisoners out in small groups to use the lavatory and fill their water pails, sounded like a round by yeomen at the Tower of London. Tramp, rattle, clang. I heard the wardress's voice from a few cells away:

'Any complaints, number two?'

Then tramp, tramp on, not pausing for an answer. A thunderous knock on my door.

'Any complaints?'

'No complaints.'

What was the use?

More tramping of feet, then my door was flung back.

'Out you come, number five. Don't hang about.'

Two wardresses in their blue uniform dresses, one young, with glossy piled-up hair, the other middle-aged, thin and nervy. I picked up my water pail from its place under the window and followed them. Each landing in the prison has lavatory cubicles with doors that don't lock and, not far away, the big tanks of more or less fresh water to which prisoners are taken, twice a day, to fill their pails with a supply for drinking and washing. Apart from chapel and the exercise yard, it's the only opportunity you get to see your fellow prisoners. You're not allowed to speak to them, of course. The rule of no talking is enforced more rigidly in Holloway than at the most strict of convent boarding schools. Even wishing another prisoner good evening – not that any evening might be good in there – would be a disciplinary offence. It was there in rules 2 and 3 of 'Regulations Relating to the Treatment and Conduct of Convicted Criminal Prisoners' that were the only decorations allowed on the walls of our cells. 'Prisoners shall observe silence. They shall not communicate or attempt to do so with one another.'

There were two other prisoners collecting their water supplies when I was escorted to the tanks, under the eye of a wardress. One was a big muscular woman I didn't recognise. The other was Violet White. Her eyes met mine, but gave nothing away except misery. The wardress told her to hurry up, she wasn't the only one in the hotel. The cloth badge on Violet's dress said DX1 2, which meant she was only three cells away from me – not that it meant much in view of the ban on communication. I dipped my pail into the tank and at the same moment Violet gave a little gasp and dropped hers, so that it clanged against the side of the tank and sank to the bottom. The wardress gave an exasperated sigh and watched as Violet reached down for it, getting her blouse wet to the elbow. No time permitted for rolling up sleeves.

I assumed that nervousness was making Violet clumsy and would have liked to help her pick up the bucket but guessed it would only make things worse. Then, as we both bent over the tank, I felt a wet pressure against my hand. Violet's wrist was pressing against mine. It was so nervy that I could feel the pulse throbbing, but the kind of nervousness that comes from determination as much as fear. As we straightened up from opposite sides of the tank, each with our full bucket, her eyes met mine again then, very purposefully, shifted to something behind me. When you're not allowed to talk other forms of communication become much stronger than usual, a kind of prison sixth-sense that comes back to you as soon as the doors slam. I knew immediately that there was something behind me that Violet wanted me to notice, but that I mustn't give her away by turning to look at once. We straightened up and turned away from each other. As we did so, she put down her pail and wiped her hand on the bodice of her blouse, just where the badge was pinned. She meant me to notice it, I was sure of that. Did she want me to know that she wasn't far away? I knew that already, besides, what was the point? She was marched back to her cell first, with a wardress still nagging away at her for being clumsy, then I was escorted back to mine.

On the way I realised what it was that Violet had wanted me to notice, although I couldn't see for the life of me why. Of the two wardresses who had opened my door, the younger one had moved on up the corridor, so only the thin middle-aged one was left to escort me. So she

42

must have been standing behind me at the water tank and Violet's urgent signal had told me to notice her. As she closed the cell door on me I gave her a long look that stopped just this side of reportable insolence, trying to see what was so important about her. She had a soured, resentful look. Her hair was thin and greying, her hands red and bony as if from too much scrubbing. In that few seconds of looking at her I knew that life had not been kind to her, so naturally she wasn't inclined to give it much kindness back. Well, there were wardresses like that. It wasn't a job you'd choose, goodness knows. But why was Violet so interested?

Alone in the cell again, I wondered about that other gesture of Violet's, the hand-wiping on the chest. It meant something, for sure. If Violet simply wanted to dry her hands, the apron would have been the natural thing to use. So she'd wanted me to notice her prison badge. Again, why? The simple fact that we were getting our water on the same landing showed that our cells must be quite close together, and she'd know I knew that. Then it came to me that it wasn't the badge at all. The point of it was that it was worn pinned to the chest at precisely the same place as you'd wear an ornamental watch, where I'd worn the watch that I'd given to Violet. She'd been trying to tell me that the watch had escaped the search when we were admitted and was still hidden and in her possession. Touching in its way, I supposed. Was it so important to her to be able to measure of the hours of her imprisonment? Were three months more tolerable counted out with garnets and small diamonds? I'd have thought that made it even worse, but then there was no predicting the way people would take prison. I was still thinking about that, as a rest from the bigger problem, when the stamping, crashing and rattling started all over again to announce the last official event of the prison day, the delivery of supper.

'Pint, number five.'

That meant you had to take your tin pint mug from its shelf and hold it out at the door for cocoa to be ladled into

43

it. That, and a not bad roll of brown bread, were supper. The cocoa hadn't changed in the time I'd been away and still had its familiar mauvish-grey tinge. After that I slept the kind of half-sleep you get in unfamiliar surroundings, punctuated by the footsteps of wardresses on their rounds. Occasionally the steps would pause in their slow rhythm and I'd hear the rasp of the cover over the spy-hole in the door being moved aside. Then they'd go on again. Once I woke to the sound of sobbing from a cell not far away. I hoped it wasn't Violet – not that I could do anything about that either.

'Visitors for you, number five. Hurry up.'

Monday morning, about ten o'clock, probably. I'd eaten my bowlful of lumpy oatmeal and water porridge, rolled up my bedding in the prescribed way, washed and polished my water pail and pint mug and stood by to have my housework inspected on the morning rounds. By normal prison routine, that should have been the end of the excitement for several hours so the arrival of two different wardresses, in a hurry as usual, was unexpected. I set my bonnet and apron straight and went as directed, one of them in front and one behind, along the corridor between the rows of closed cell doors and down an iron circular staircase. Then the leading wardress unlocked a door and we were briefly out in the air, between the cliff-like sides of two cell blocks. Even after only one day of being locked up it was good to breathe the air, but it didn't last long. In at another door, up two flights of stone stairs, along another corridor. This one had a strip of coconut matting down the middle of it and the light came in through windows of ordinary clear glass, not the thick ribbed kind of the cell blocks. This luxury suggested that we were in an administrative wing where prisoners did not normally go. I couldn't remember it from my other times there and wondered what was going on.

When the wardress said 'visitors' I'd allowed myself to hope, just for a second, that it might be a friend to see me. It would have been a surprise because I knew

I wasn't entitled to a visit at the start of a sentence. I remembered the casual, almost unconscious cruelty practised on prisoners by the system that holds them and crushed the hope as soon as it formed. Just as well. I'd met the two people waiting in the room that I was taken to, but I could hardly describe them as friends. One was the young labrador-faced plain-clothes man who'd questioned me at Scotland Yard and went by the name of Brust. The other, in police uniform, was a slightly older acquaintance.

'Good morning, Inspector Merit.'

He began to stand up, caught Brust's cold eye and sat down again hastily.

'I'm sorry to see you here, Miss Bray.'

A stir from the two wardresses standing behind me. In here, I wasn't supposed to be 'Miss'. Inspector Merit told them that they could go.

'I don't suppose Miss Bray intends to dive out of the window.'

From the look Mr Brust was giving me, I thought he wasn't too sure of that, but he made no protest as the wardresses withdrew, closing the door behind them.

I said to Inspector Merit, 'I'm glad you're here.'

Which was true, up to a point. If there had to be a policeman, it might as well be this one. Our paths had crossed once before when he'd suspected me of harbouring a murder suspect. He'd been wrong at the time, but near enough right to make it uncomfortable. Later, when the case had been cleared up more or less to his satisfaction, he was fair-minded enough to say that he didn't approve of my methods but I might have saved him from making a mistake. He had a pouchy, anxious face and a way of stretching the skin on his temples with his fingertips when worried. He began doing it now, as he sat down and I guessed that he distrusted the plain-clothes man and disliked working with him. I was struck again by this inexplicable air of superiority about Brust. He was at least ten years younger than Merit and, at that age, could hardly outrank him, but there was a sense of puffy

45

importance about him, as if he knew things not divulged to the man in uniform.

I said, 'There was something I should have told you on Saturday evening. I forgot it then and only remembered it later.'

He looked at me. His small eyes folded into disbelieving slits.

'Forgot it, did you?'

'That blue-dyed sheet that was used to cover the body, it came off the cart. I remember noticing at the time that it had some kind of monogram woven into it. The letters weren't from the usual alphabet and I thought perhaps they might be Russian. I suppose you'll still have the sheet at Scotland Yard so you could check.'

Merit glanced towards Brust, who seemed totally unimpressed.

'And was there anything else you forgot to tell us on Saturday night?'

'I don't think so. Naturally I've been thinking a lot about it since, but I don't think there was anything else.'

I was still standing.

'Sit down,' Merit said.

I took the single chair that was left, facing them across a battered desk with a well-used blotting pad.

'Something else about the float, maybe?'

'No, I'm sorry.'

It was obvious, from the way he was looking at me and Merit was looking at him that Brust held a significant card. I felt as uneasy as I was probably meant to feel.

'You told us on Saturday that you hadn't seen it before.'

'I hadn't. I only noticed it for the first time on the bridge.'

'And decided there was something odd about it?'

'Yes.'

'What about Mr Frater. Did he think there was something odd about it, too?'

'No, I don't think so. He only noticed because I pointed it out to him.'

'So to the best of your knowledge he'd never seen it before either?'

'I'm quite sure he'd never seen it before.'

Brust opened a notepad on the desk and took his time writing that down. I knew I was meant to feel intimidated, but the infuriating thing was that it worked. My sense that something was about to be sprung on me was growing. Merit didn't like it. If he went on stretching at his skin like that he'd have it down in folds over his ears. Brust stopped writing and sighed.

'We discussed Mr Frater on Saturday night, didn't we?'

'I told you that he was quite incapable of murdering anybody.'

'You directed my attention to a book he'd written. With some difficulty, I obtained a copy of the book. I spent a large part of yesterday evening studying it.'

I wondered what alarmed bookseller had been summoned to his premises on a Sunday afternoon to provide Scotland Yard with a history of Roman politics, written mainly for undergraduates.

'Have you read the book in question?'

'Yes.'

In fact, I'd helped him proof-read it. Brust made another note.

'What can you tell me about Mr Frater's political opinions?'

'What's that got to do with it?'

'Answer my question.'

I decided it could do no harm to Simon.

'He's not attached to any political party. In fact, he refuses even to use his vote until women are given the vote as well.'

'Has he ever talked in your presence of assassination?'

'Has he what?'

I nearly fell off the chair.

'Assassination. The prime minister, for instance, or even the king?'

47

'No, of course he hasn't. He's the last man in the world to think of assassinating anybody.'

'You say you've read his book. Including chapter twelve?'

'Of course I've read chapter twelve. That's the . . . oh, my god.'

Light began to dawn, but the kind of light that might as well be darkness.

'Yes?' Brust was looking at me, wide nostrils twitching. 'You were going to say . . .?'

I said nothing.

'Perhaps I should remind you that chapter twelve deals with Julius Caesar. The assassination of Julius Caesar.'

If he'd punched me in the stomach I couldn't have been more taken aback. It was some time before I managed to say anything.

'I hope you're not going to imply that an academic discussion of something that happened two thousand years ago makes a man a murder suspect.'

'In itself, no.'

It was no good telling myself not to get angry. I was past the point of listening to my own advice.

'In itself, nothing. It's pure craziness to regard it as evidence of anything.'

Merit was shaking his head a little, I didn't know whether at Brust or me. Brust took no notice.

'He lists, as you may remember, several reasons why the conspirators might have felt themselves justified in killing Julius Caesar.'

'Of course he does. You'll remember he also lists some reasons why it might not have been a good idea. For heaven's sake, Shakespeare gives the conspirators some good lines too. Would you have arrested him on suspicion of murder?'

'As far as I know, Mr Shakespeare was never discovered beside a carnival float standing over a dead body with a gun in his hand.'

I sat there and stared at him. Mistakes you can argue

with, but when you collide with something as brick-wall wrong-headed as that, all you can do is try to stop your head spinning.

'Are you seriously suggesting that Simon Frater would carry out a random killing of a man he'd never met before because of a Roman constitutional theory?'

'How do you know it was random?'

'I don't suppose he'd ever met Robert Withering.'

I threw in the name quite deliberately. He hadn't yet told me the identity of the dead man and I thought it was probably one of the cards he was waiting to play and watch its effect on me. Two could play at that. As I'd expected, he pounced heavily.

'How did you know who it was?'

'It must have been common knowledge by Sunday morning. A friend visited me in the police cells and told me.'

I could see he was disappointed about that, but there was still the air of smugness about him. Now I had time to think I was a little reassured. If that smugness was based on nothing more than an idiotic interpretation of Simon's book, it couldn't be such a serious threat.

'Did you know Mr Withering?'

That question, in more reasonable tones, came from Inspector Merit. I turned to him, trying to shut Brust out.

'No. I know of his father, although I've never met him.'

'Did you and Mr Frater disapprove of his father's political views?'

'Some of them, yes, but not to the extent of wanting to assassinate his son.'

Brust said to Merit, from over my shoulder: 'Aren't we getting side-tracked, Inspector?' Then, to me: 'You say you hadn't seen that cart before Saturday evening?'

'I hadn't.'

'Nor any of the things on it?'

'No.'

'So you had no idea what was on that vehicle?'

49

'Apart from what I could see, no.'

Brust sat back, as if I'd conceded an important point. He said to Merit, 'Apart from what she could see.' Then repeated the phrase several times, sounding more sceptical each time. Merit looked uneasy. I waited.

'And what about the things you couldn't see?'

'If I couldn't see them, I could hardly be aware of them.'

'You'll concede that there might have been things on that vehicle not immediately visible to a spectator.'

'Of course. The faces of the people under the masks, for a start.'

'Oh, we weren't talking about faces, were we? We weren't talking about faces.'

Again that smug look towards an unresponsive Merit. I began to get a prickling in my skin, a feeling that we were coming at last to the point he'd been aiming for all along. He was waiting for me to ask a question. I didn't.

He hitched himself forward in his chair, leaning at me across the desk.

'Do you happen to recall what the king figure was sitting on?'

I thought about it.

'Some kind of low dais or podium. You couldn't see what it was because it was covered with red, white and blue draperies. I suppose if I'd thought about it at all, I'd have guessed it was built of crates or boxes.'

'Boxes. Several boxes.'

He said it as if it were part of a case against me.

'The question is, what was in those boxes?'

The eyes were no more than slits, but bright as electric light bulbs.

'Since you've only just informed me there were boxes, you can hardly expect me to guess what they contained.'

He waited. Looked at me, looked at Merit, at the ceiling. I realised that I was on the edge of my chair, playing his game and made myself sit back.

'Well, don't you want to know? Or perhaps you know already?'

'No.'

Another wait, then he spoke quite softly. 'Dynamite.' The eyes were on me, not blinking. He said the word again, caressing it as if it were something precious.

'Enough dynamite to blow up half Whitehall. But you wouldn't know about that, I suppose.'

SIX

A CLOCK ON THE WALL behind me creaked and ticked. Feet went past outside. I concentrated on them, quick and official, padding into the distance on the coconut matting. I counted twenty ticks of the clock, making myself keep my eyes on his.

'You don't seem very surprised.'

'Appearances are deceptive, then. I am surprised.'

'You didn't know?'

I looked at Inspector Merit.

'Is he telling the truth?'

Merit nodded slowly. He'd stopped trying to stretch the skin over his skull, but his eyes looked sad. I thought that although I couldn't count him on my side, he didn't want to be on Brust's either.

'We found the cart up a side street in Lambeth. It had been abandoned. When we searched it there was a stack of dynamite under the podium in the middle.'

'Ye gods. It was on fire. I told you, I saw the executioner trying to stamp it out.'

He nodded.

'The fuse was coiled up round the side of the podium, quite a long fuse, to give them time to get clear, I suppose. If somebody hadn't managed to put the flames out it would have caught and . . . well, there'd have been a big hole in Westminster Bridge.'

I stared at him. Brust took over the conversation again, seeming annoyed that Merit had told me so much.

'Did you know there was dynamite on the cart?'

52

'I'll assume what you've told me is true. The answer is, I didn't know. I had no reason to know.'

'So you say.'

I let myself lose my temper then. The tension in me had to go somewhere.

'For heaven's sake, are you seriously suggesting I'd escort a cart loaded with dynamite up to the front doors of Scotland Yard?'

'You threw a brick through the Prime Minister's window once.'

'That was different. That was a political protest. Dynamite kills people, innocent people.'

'There are those who seem to think that's a price worth paying.'

'I'm not one of them, and neither is Simon, nor anybody else in the suffragette movement. This couldn't be anything to do with any of us.'

'You were an official march steward.'

The realisation of what my action might mean, not only for Simon and myself but for the movement as a whole, was beginning to flood over me, wave after wave. There were idiots out there who'd think we were quite capable of trying to blow up Scotland Yard or the Houses of Parliament.

'It was nothing to do with us. Somebody was trying to use us and our march.'

And like the fool I was, in suspecting something like that and trying to prevent it, I'd made it worse. If I thought about that too much, with Brust looking at me, I'd do or say something that would dig a deeper pit. The only thing I could do to help everybody was try to stay calm and, if this man was beyond convincing, at least to learn as much as I could.

'Anarchists?'

Brust said nothing.

'You remember I told you on Saturday night that I'd heard the driver cursing in what might have been a Baltic language.'

No reaction from Brust. I turned to Inspector Merit.

53

'It might have been Latvian. Suppose the whole thing were meant as revenge for Sidney Street. Blowing up Scotland Yard might have seemed appropriate to them.'

Merit said, 'It's by no means certain that was the aim. There were a number of potential targets on your procession route.'

Brust gave him a warning look.

'She may know more about that than we do.'

'Are you charging me with conspiracy to dynamite?'

'All in good time.'

'If you thought I knew about that dynamite, a good time would be now.'

'Do you want me to?'

'No. But I won't play this cat and mouse game forever. Either charge me with murder or planning to blow up Scotland Yard, or whatever you're pretending to think I did or . . .' I stopped.

'Or what?'

It was Brust's best moment in the interview. His voice when he said the two words was a kind of porcine purr. Because he knew what I'd intended to say. My next words should have been something on the lines of '. . . or I'll walk out here and now and you can send for me when you've finally made up your mind'. I think I may even have started to stand up until the sliding of my feet in the worn, shapeless shoes reminded me where I was and what I was. I'd never felt so totally the consciousness of being a prisoner.

'Or what?' he repeated.

'Or we can discuss it without threats like sensible human beings. I'm as anxious to find out who killed Robert Withering as you are, and as much opposed to dynamiters.'

I was trying to think it through. Assuming that it was true about the dynamite, the plan of the people on the float must have been to wait until it was alongside the target building, then light the fuse and retire hastily. If Scotland Yard had been their object, then they were within a minute or two of doing that when Withering was shot. Risky, but not impossible. With reasonable luck the conspirators would get clear before the dynamite exploded, just as they'd got away after the shot. No time to unhitch the poor old horse from his shafts, though, which explained why they'd given the duty to such a tired old beast. He was expendable.

'What happened to the horse?'

Brust looked puzzled, but Merit got the point.

'He's in the police pound.'

'Has anyone looked for a brand mark on him, or a number on his hoof? There might be a record of a sale somewhere.'

Brust's face went red.

'May I remind you that you're not conducting this investigation.'

'No, but unless you're going to charge me, I'm voluntarily helping you with your inquiries.'

He glanced towards the closed door, at a bell push beside him on the desk.

'All right, you can keep me in here but you can't do more than that. If you really want my help, then you might start by being honest with me.'

'Honest! Honest with her! Just listen to her.'

Brust, snorting, appealed to Merit but got no reaction. His face was now the colour of a peony petal and almost as shiny. He banged the side of his fist on the blotter.

'Now you look here, my good woman, if you go on like this you'll find yourself in serious trouble. If you're hiding something from us . . .'

He put the rest of it into a glare. I glared back.

'Firstly, my good man, I'm not hiding anything from you because I don't know anything. As for serious trouble, it can't be much worse than being in Holloway suspected of knowingly escorting a cart of dynamite up to the doors of Scotland Yard. The help I'm offering is nothing more than a modest addition to your collective brain-power. If that worries you, then I'm sorry but I can't do anything about it.'

Poor Merit had his head in his hands by now. If he'd

been dragged along because of his experience in dealing with me, he seemed ready to resign his speciality.

'I'm sorry,' I said to his bent head, 'I'm trying, I really am.'

He raised his head and looked at me.

'What did you mean about being honest with you?'

Brust snorted something about not taking any notice of her. I ignored him.

'About what young Withering was doing. You tell me that cart had dynamite on it. We agree, I think, that if so it might well have been an anarchist bombing attempt. What doesn't make sense is that the son of a Liberal cabinet minister was mixed up in it.'

Merit looked down at the blotter.

'What was he doing there? I can guess, but I'm sure you two don't have to guess.'

Brust said, 'Don't get into a discussion with her.'

Again, Merit ignored him.

'You say you can guess. What do you guess?'

'There's no point in asking her . . .'

'I think Robert Withering must have been working for you, for the police. He'd managed to become a trusted member of an anarchist group and was sending you information. Somehow he didn't manage to get information to you beforehand about the bombing attempt. He'd have been in a terrible position, poor man. Here he was, part of a team going to blow up Scotland Yard, wondering how to stop it at the last minute. Somehow, as that cart turned off the bridge, he must have tried. Perhaps he took the risk of starting the fire himself, hoping it would scare the others into abandoning the cart. Perhaps he was trying to stop somebody else lighting the fuse and a match got dropped. Then one of the gang saw what was going on and shot him.'

I'd almost forgotten where I was again, in the excitement of reconstructing it and Brust was reminding me with a hostile stare.

'Then poor Simon, knowing no more of all this than I did, clambers up onto the cart at exactly the wrong moment. Pity your people didn't follow it when I told them to.'

Silence. More footsteps going past outside. In the end it was Inspector Merit who answered.

'It's an ingenious theory. I'm afraid it has one big defect. Young Mr Withering was never working for Scotland Yard.'

He was trying to believe me, so I tried to believe him. The best I could manage was to think that he was not deliberately lying.

'Would you know for sure if he were?'

Such operations would come under a relatively new department of Scotland Yard called the Special Branch. I'd heard that the men in it – and I was sure that Brust was one – were a law unto themselves.

Brust said flatly, 'He wasn't working for us.'

'Could it have been some sort of freelance organisation? Had he been in the army, for instance?'

Brust declined to take any further interest. Merit glanced at him.

'No. I don't see any harm in telling you that Robert had been a considerable anxiety to his father. He was to have entered the diplomatic corps. After Cambridge he went to Paris and Geneva to improve his languages, but he got into some pretty odd company there. His father didn't even know he was back in the country, so this has come as a considerable shock to him.'

'You mean he might really have taken up with anarchists?'

'Yes.'

I wasn't convinced. It seemed to be far more likely, even assuming they were telling me the truth about his not being a police spy, that he'd been engaged in the sort of freelance adventure that wealthy young men do go in for from time to time. Still, it was generous of Merit to tell me the story because it supported my side of things.

'So, even by Scotland Yard's account, we have a cart loaded with dynamite and masked anarchists, along with a well-born young man who may have acquired some sinister friends. Then when the predictable thing happens and they fall out among themselves and take to shooting, you let them get away and arrest poor innocent Simon, who had no more to do with it than he had with the assassination of Julius Caesar. Surely you can see that now.'

Brust heaved a deep sigh.

'I thought I'd made it clear that you're not here to lecture us.'

'What am I here for then? To prop up your half-baked theories, when you've arrested the wrong person and won't look for the right ones?'

'You're here because we're trying to help you out of the trouble you've got yourself into.'

He planted his elbows on the desk and lowered his chin onto his hands, training the narrow slits of his eyes on me.

'You've got two choices. Either you help me, and I do what I can for you, or you don't, in which case . . .'

'Well?'

'. . . in which case, it's not just thirty days in Holloway we're talking about.'

I've met most varieties of bullying, but for all the crudeness of it there was something about this one that made me go cold. He wasn't imposing. The body was more pulpy than powerful, the brain inconsiderable and yet somehow that didn't prevent him from being threatening. A hippopotamus in a mud wallow has the same quality, ridiculous little eyes, big nostrils and thick baggy hide. And yet let it come out of its wallow, flaring its nostrils, waddling on its stumpy legs and if you've got any sense you run for it or climb a tree. I couldn't climb or run. I stared at him, he stared at me and it seemed to go on for a long time. When at last he touched the bell on his desk and a wardress came to take me back to my cell, I was even pleased to see her.

SEVEN

LOCKED UP AGAIN, I HAD more time than I wanted to think. I was scared – which was nothing new – but scared in a way I'd never been before. The interview with Brust had shaken something I'd taken for granted, but it took me some time to understand what exactly it was. I nagged away at it in the interval between the stamping and crashing that brought lunch (cold beef and warmish potatoes with the bad bits left in) and the next stamping and crashing when we were escorted to the lavatories and water tanks. I got there in the end. What he had undermined was the belief in the essential decency and fairness of the system of justice.

All right, I'd seen it make mistakes and had spent more time than I wanted trying to correct some of them. But I'd always assumed that though a guilty person might get convicted by accident, there was never an intention among police or judges to do it deliberately. Point out the mistake convincingly enough and the mistake would be put right – always assuming that the innocent person hadn't been hanged in the mean time. What was new this time was the certainty that some people involved in this case knew perfectly well that Simon Frater had not shot Robert Withering, but were determined to pretend that he did. Once you allowed that as a possibility, the floorboards gave way and you were stepping into emptiness, with the smell of fungoid things waiting down in the basement.

I paced up and down for a long time, trying to get used to that smell, until it struck me that there was a kind of hope there too. At one point in the interview, when Brust had

59

been talking about Julius Caesar, I'd thought he was simply a very stupid man. That had been worrying, because you can't do anything about stupidity. It just lies there across the path and refuses to be moved. Cleverness, on the other hand, is mobile. It twists and turns, dodges and tries to trip you up. If you move faster and manoeuvre more skilfully, you can get past it. I could have done nothing against Brust's stupidity, but surely I could defeat his cleverness. It was a matter of working out what he wanted, and the fact that he'd bothered to come out to Holloway with Merit in tow suggested that he wanted something very much.

I was certain that the unfortunate Withering had been engaged in some kind of spying mission against the anarchists, that he'd died as a result and that for some reason they were determined to obscure the facts. Why they wanted to do it, I didn't know. It was possible that Withering's work was part of a wider scheme that hadn't reached its conclusion yet. In that case, it might suit them to hold Simon for the murder only as a temporary measure, to lull the real murderer into a sense of security. But I couldn't be sure of that and even if I did know it for sure the fact remained that an innocent man was in prison, and probably in real fear for his life, because of something in which I'd got him involved.

At half-past seven cocoa comes round again. At nine they turn the lights out. That is, the feeble gas jet that burns behind a panel of thick ribbed glass high up in the cell wall goes out with a pop and complete darkness falls over you. After the first few minutes you realise that it isn't quite complete because a little light filters in from the corridor around the edges of the cover over the spy-hole, but there's not enough of it to see your own hand by, let alone write or read. I imagined the same happening to Simon in Wormwood Scrubs or wherever they'd put him and guessed that for him, with his naturally restless mind, the worst part of the day would just be starting. It takes practice to deal with the boredom of being in prison. He had no practice and no natural talent for it. One of my worries was that he'd break down and do something desperate that would make things even worse for him – if they could be worse. It was all very well to tell myself, as I did, that they couldn't try, sentence and hang Simon in the twenty-nine days it would take me to get out of prison. Twenty-nine days on remand for a murder you didn't commit would drive anybody mad. Suppose they made him so confused or depressed that he even confessed to doing it. Anything I or anybody else might do to help him would be nearly useless then.

It must have been the early hours of the morning before I worked myself to that particular worry. In the dark, without a watch, there was no way of telling for sure, but I knew a wardress had already patrolled our corridor twice since the lights went out, sliding in the soft-soled shoes they wear not to protect prisoners' sleep but in the hope of catching them trying to communicate between their cells. It was some time after the second round, when the place had gone as quiet as it ever goes, that the knocking on the pipes started. At first you might have taken it for intestinal disturbances of the heating pipes that ran through every cell, except that this was summer so the heating system was turned off. Soft little knocking sounds that you wouldn't have noticed by day, as if knuckles were rapping gently and cautiously against the thick cast iron pipe. I knew that was exactly what was happening. Tapping on those big pipes that run through Holloway like veins was one way of communication among prisoners. Sometimes before big suffragette demonstrations, when groups of us knew we were likely to get arrested together, we'd even work out a kind of rough code in advance. Each woman would have an identifying signal, plus other groups of taps, with intervals long or short, representing useful words. If you had time and patience to learn morse code in advance, that was even better.

I lay back on my plank bed and listened. I didn't expect any of the messages to be for me, since as far as I knew there were no other suffragette prisoners in that block, but

I couldn't help trying to make some sense out of them. Whoever was trying to communicate was being very persistent, with the same rhythm being repeated time after time, first a flurry of little taps, then five taps slow and deliberate, with the space of a breath between each, then a longer space, then two taps. She must have sent it at least half a dozen times before I noticed the pattern which was risky, both because it might attract the attention of the wardresses or annoy other prisoners who didn't want to join the game. As a relief from the bigger problem, I began wondering what it was that somebody wanted to say so desperately. It took another three repetitions before I connected the constantly repeated five taps with the number of my own cell. Once I'd got that, there was no problem in guessing the rest. The two taps stood for cell number two, Violet's.

This was not good news. I knew Violet was depressed and lonely and felt sorry for her, but didn't want to add the risks of forbidden communication to my problems unless it was going to be some use. For two more repetitions of that steady, desperate rhythm I tried to ignore it, but then the terrible loneliness of the tapping, like a last solitary woodpecker in some metallic copse at the end of the world, was too much for me. I got up, knelt down by the pipe along the wall, and tapped out on it my response, as softly as I could: first the flurry of little taps to show I was there, then two taps for her address, five taps for mine. There was a few seconds' silence, then a positive flurry of small taps that needed no translation. Yes, yes, yes. Here you are at last. What kept you? In answer I struck the pipe twice with my palm, as softly as I could, hoping it might convey the message: calm down.

It worked to the extent that the next communication was calmer, three deliberate beats, then a harder beat. One, two, three, NOW. One, two, three, NOW. I couldn't make head or tail of that, struck one questioning beat. The signal was repeated, again and again. Experimentally, I tried echoing it in reply: tap, tap, tap, TAP. Instantly came that dancing flurry of small, excited taps. Yes, yes, yes. Violet was pleased I'd got the message at last. The only problem was, I'd no idea what the message was supposed to be. I struck the pipe again with my palm, hoping to convey a question mark. What I got instead was a heavy and annoyed thump on the wall dividing me from cell number four next door. This took no trouble to decode. My neighbour was displeased with these nocturnal goings on and wished us both to be quiet before the wardresses came and started making trouble for all of us. I had some sympathy with her and besides you don't quarrel with your neighbours in prison. I gave the pipe one last goodnight tap and then lay down with the scratchy blanket pulled up over my ears. Violet repeated her incomprehensible message just once more, then there was silence more or less until, just after six o'clock, the shuffling of the wardresses' night footwear gave place to the stamping and rattling of the Holloway dawn chorus.

That day, Tuesday, was like any other prison day apart from what was going round in my head. During the morning, when a senior wardress came on the usual cursory tour to ask if there were any complaints, I said I wanted to see my solicitor. The reason I gave her was that I was worried about my investments because I knew that the penal system, tender about very few things, has a scrupulous reverence for business interests. She duly made a note of it and I didn't see fit to mention that my investments amounted to a handful of more or less unprofitable Scottish ferry shares left to me by my father. The idea was that if I could only have a visit from somebody I might use the opportunity, even under the eye of a wardress, to get out what I guessed about the activities of the late Robert Withering. It was a faint hope, even at best, and I knew I couldn't expect a response to my request for a week at least because it would have to go up to the governor. But at least it was an attempt to do something and without that I think I'd have gone mad from frustration and impatience. There were times when I thought I was anyway. Because I'd only been in the place for a day and a half I wasn't yet scheduled for sessions in the exercise yard or the workrooms. My world was the cell, the 'Regulations Relating to the Treatment and Conduct of Convicted Criminal Prisoners' on the wall, the Bible, hymn book and prayer book stacked on the shelf by the thick-paned window, the tin mug and plate on another shelf. Once I'd rolled up my bedding in the prescribed Swiss-roll fashion with the sheets on the inside, washed and polished plate and mug in the water pail with the cloth provided and stood by my bed for inspection, that was the end of the day's official activity. I tried to set up a scheme of exercises for myself as I'd done on past visits – so many paces up and down the cell, arm swings as far as the space allowed, stretching and toe-touching. This time it didn't work. It seemed ridiculous, frivolous, to be worrying about personal fitness. The result was that by the time the gas went out at nine o'clock I was feeling further from sleep than I'd ever done in my life.

At various times in the long day I'd thought of Violet's message along the pipes and thought I'd worked out what she was saying. She'd been counting out her sentence of three months. One-two-three OUT. That bothered me, as far as I had any space in my mind for worrying about anything other than Simon and Brust. Still only two days into a ninety-day sentence, she'd go mad with impatience if she looked at it like that. I hoped she wouldn't find it necessary to tap out the same message tonight but, sure enough, after the wardresses' soft-shoed round, it started again. First the five taps, then that same insistent beat. I'd decided to ignore it. If she kept on like this she'd be discovered and would lose any chance of remission of her sentence. Kinder not to answer her so that she got discouraged and stopped trying. But even with the bedding pulled over my head, the metallic woodpecker still penetrated.

After a while it struck me that it wasn't that same rhythm as the night before. Instead of three regularly spaced taps, followed by the harder NOW it was two regular taps then the louder one. One, two, NOW. One, two, NOW. Among other annoyances, this made nonsense of my guess that she was counting off the months to release. I willed her to stop, but she wouldn't. My neighbour thumped the wall again, but she still went on. In the end, cursing Violet in my mind, I decided that the only way to silence her was to let her know that I'd heard the message, whatever it might be. I waited for her to signal again, then repeated it along the pipe, tap for tap, along with the palm-thump that I hoped would tell her to be quiet now. It worked. The tapping stopped and I managed a few hours of broken sleep, but woke up in the early hours of Wednesday morning, still with no idea of what Violet was trying to say to me. One thing clear was that if she were measuring time, she was counting in days not months. On Tuesday morning something had been three days away, on Wednesday two. Two more days then something. The day after next would be Friday and after some thought – cut off already from the outside world – I remembered Friday was the day the King was being crowned. Surely Violet hadn't caught coronation fever to add to all her other problems. I was beginning to have grave doubts about her mental stability.

Even in Holloway preparations for the coronation didn't pass us by entirely but filtered through in the only way they could, via the wardresses. From scraps of their conversations overheard as they were superintending us on the landings or pausing with the food carts at our doors, we gathered that an almighty row was in progress over leave rotas for the big day. Everybody, naturally, wanted at least half a day off for the processions and street parties. Rank was being pulled, pleas made, umbrage taken. Our bread rolls came flying at us through the doorways, cocoa slopped into mugs as the debates went on over our silent, white-bonneted heads.

On Wednesday our guards were arguing about it when I was allowed out into the yard for exercise. About a dozen of us were there at the same time, pacing round in a circle with at least five yards in between us and several wardresses watching intently to make sure that we didn't try to communicate with each other. I was glad that Violet White wasn't in the same batch for exercise, given her passion for illicit communication. One of the wardresses, standing on her own, was the resentful-looking middle-aged woman Violet had been so anxious I should notice that first night on the landing, keeping a little apart from the others and looking as cheerless as usual. On one of my circuits I glanced up at her as I passed and found her looking intently at me. Our eyes collided rather than met. She looked away at once, which was odd for a wardress, and yet I somehow had the impression that she'd been watching me for quite a long time. You might say that was her job, after all, and yet the others weren't watching us individually as I thought this one – Misery Minny I'd tagged her in my mind – had been watching me. Their gazes ranged over the whole trudging circle of us, seeing that the pattern of green-dressed prisoners and grey spaces was according to regulations, but hardly aware of us as individuals at all. It came to me that Misery Minny might be under instructions from somebody, like Brust say, to keep a special watch on me and report back to him. Once I thought that, I could feel her eyes between my shoulder-blades as I walked, like the touch of cold fingers.

That night, Wednesday night, there was no knocking on the pipes. The next morning began in the usual routine, but some time after the bed inspection, probably around ten o'clock, there was an extra outbreak of noise and, from the floor below us, the sound of a lot of people moving around. Then it was our turn, doors being rattled open in a hurry, wardresses shouting.

'Hurry up. Chapel. Hymn books and prayer books.'

As we went in crocodile down the staircase the news got back along the line that it was a special service, to pray for the king at his coronation next day. It gives some idea of the suffocating boredom of prison life that most of the line seemed to regard this as moderately good news. Even chapel was better than a cell. Somebody once remarked to me that there are no atheists in prison, but that's more a proof of sociability than religious instinct.

We were chivvied into high-backed pews, with wardresses snapping at anybody who got carried away by the excitement and tried to whisper to her neighbour. We'd formed up in lines according to our block, corridor and cell numbers which meant that Violet was separated from me by only two prisoners. On the way into the chapel she'd shown no sign of noticing me, but as we filed into a pew there was a little scuffle ahead of me and when we sat down, Violet had managed to manoeuvre herself into the place beside me. Her sharp elbow dug into my ribs, but her eyes were cast down piously. She opened one of the two books she was carrying and appeared to be studying it.

'Stand up.'

A sharp command from the front. One of the trusted prisoners – trusted for her conduct, that is, rather than her musical sense – began to play something by Handel on the harmonium, giving it a trudging rhythm. As we stood up the dignitaries came in and took their places close to the altar, the governor, the chaplain, a couple of male visiting magistrates in stiff collars and dark suits. The chaplain ascended the pulpit and the governor and magistrates took their seats beside it. They'd have been looking at a white-capped sea of green and brown prison outfits, except they kept their eyes elevated above it, as if watching for something better to come over the horizon. Facing them, in an upper gallery, were more prisoners and wardresses. At our level a few wardresses sat in the aisles, with their backs to the altar and the line of dignitaries, watching us. This meant we were sandwiched between observers at two levels. The pressure of Violet's elbow in my ribs increased. I tried not to respond.

'Let us pray.'

We sank to our knees. Violet already had her prayer book open, propped on the ledge behind the pew in front of us, and was studying it devotedly. I wondered if she might be developing religious mania.

'Dear Lord, who seest the inmost secrets of our hearts . . .'

She had her finger on something, was prodding away at my ribs with her elbow. To try to keep her quiet, I looked at where she was pointing. First surprise, it wasn't the prayer book she had there at all, it was the Bible. She must have snatched up the wrong one from the shelf in her cell when we were hustled out. And yet there was something there I was supposed to notice. It was the story of the children of Israel in bondage in Egypt. Appropriate enough in a way, I suppose, but not much help to us. Did she think we should be praying for swarms of locusts and plagues of frogs to descend on Holloway until they relented and let us go? That might be about as useful as anything else I could think of at the moment. I gave her what was meant to be a little reassuring nod, but felt her body quivering with annoyance. It seemed I hadn't got the point. As the chaplain prayed Violet's finger went sliding up to the top of the page and its heading: The Book of Exodus. I nodded again, meaning, yes, nice joke, now for goodness' sake stop making trouble. More quivering. Her finger tapped at a word. Exodus. Exodus. Exodus.

What could I do? I'd already seen something of her fear of being locked up again. If she was like this after five days, three months of it would drive her mad. In other circumstances I'd have made a note to nag at the wardresses until they got a doctor to see her, but with Simon to think about I couldn't afford to use up any spare goodwill there might be for Violet. But her finger went on tapping away as if it were a ritual to summon up the thing she was craving. I glanced sideways at her face. She caught my eye and nodded, registering that I'd got the message at last. After that she stayed quiet through a reading about King David by another trusted prisoner and a sermon by the chaplain, in which he exhorted us to think about the responsibilities our new king would be taking upon himself and how we all, in our more humble spheres, should shoulder the burden of responsibility, be it light or heavy, which God had seen fit we should carry through life.

I sensed that the mood of the meeting wasn't with him, and whatever kept his listeners awake at night it wasn't likely to be worry about the responsibilities of King George V. It reminded me of one of the realities of prison that you forget mercifully soon after you're out of it, that far worse than the loneliness or the boredom or the food, is having to listen to people in authority talking nonsense and not being allowed to answer. On our knees for another set of prayers, then on our feet for a hymn. 'Now Thank We All Our God', with the introduction on the harmonium sounding as slow as prison hours. We launched into the first verse. One of the visiting magistrates seemed concerned at our lack of opportunity to hear a deep male voice at full throttle and was doing his best to make it up to us.

'. . . with hearts and hands and voices . . .'

The wardress sitting closest to us, a pretty woman in her twenties, responded by lifting her head and letting fly in a pure chorister's soprano.

'Who wondrous things has done . . .'

'Nell.'

Violet's quiet voice, close to my ear.

'Nell, understand?' Sharp and urgent.

'Who from our mothers' arms . . .'

The hymn surged slowly round us, gathering force.

'Tomorrow. Just do what she says.'

'. . . still is ours today.'

End of verse. Time for everybody to shuffle and get their breath. The pretty wardress gave a quick glance along our line then, as the harmonium played the introductory note for the next verse, tilted her chin and soared off into song again.

'Oh may this bounteous God . . .'

'Could be any time, but afternoon probably.'

'. . . ever joyful hearts . . .'

'Understand?'

I pretended to be singing. Violet had a clever way of sliding her voice at me just as everybody around us launched onto the loud notes.

69

'And keep us in His grace . . .'
'Nell, do you understand?'
'And guide us when perplexed . . .'
'Just nod if you understand.'

Perplexed was right. If I didn't let her know I understood, she'd try something more desperate. I nodded and felt her relax a little.

'And free us from all ills/In this world and the next.'

As we sat down at the end of the hymn her hand brushed against mine. I think she might even have meant it to be reassuring. It wasn't.

EIGHT

BACK IN THE CELL, I replaced prayer and hymn books on the shelf in their prescribed orderly manner and wondered what in the world to do about it. Violet, against all the odds, had succeeded in making her meaning all too clear. She was making an escape attempt. It was to be the very next day. With entirely unwanted generosity she was including me. There might even be a third one because she'd told me, 'Do what she says.' The wardress Misery Minny came into it somewhere, perhaps as the worst threat, which was worrying in itself considering I was sure she'd been watching me particularly in the exercise yard. Worst of all, Violet seemed to have left no room for doubt that I'd join her.

It might seem odd that though I'd wanted with every nerve in my body to be out of Holloway so that I could help Simon, escape had never occurred to me. For one thing, it seemed nearly impossible and I could think of no cases where it had been done successfully. For another, it was one of those things you didn't do. You challenged society, so society locked you up and you hoped that if enough of you went on doing it long enough then your legislators would see how ridiculous the whole thing was becoming. Escaping from prison would entirely destroy the point. I paced up and down, arguing it out with myself. This time I hadn't set out to get myself in prison. I was quite sure that I was not guilty as charged therefore might be said to have a right to regain my liberty. Specious, but not entirely convincing even to me. There were, after all, less drastic methods of protesting innocence. No, if there was any good reason for escaping it would be my suspicion that the police weren't playing by the rules in their treatment of Simon and me, so any obligation to be an obedient prisoner could be set aside.

I accepted, for the moment at least, that this was fair enough and went on to the next stage. Suppose I did join Violet's escape attempt. By far the most likely outcome was that we'd be discovered before we even got as far as the stairs. I didn't know what the penalties were for trying to escape because it hadn't arisen before but I thought they'd probably involve months or even years more in prison. Then there was the damage the publicity would do the cause. '*Suffragette in prison escape plot.*' The headline writers wouldn't concern themselves with the moral rights or wrongs. Worst of all, any slim hope that the police or courts might listen to me would be gone entirely. Who'd believe an escaped convict? Suppose, against all expectation, that the attempt worked and we found ourselves outside. How could I carry out any kind of investigation if I were on the run myself? I couldn't even approach any of my friends for help without involving the movement. At the very best I might manage to contact some friendly solicitor – and I could just imagine his look of horror if I did – but there was nothing I could tell him that would make it worth this kind of risk.

No. Much though I regretted it, the answer to Violet had to be no, no, no. But how could I deliver it? I could hardly send a note along the corridor. '*Miss Bray regrets that she is unable to accept Miss White's kind invitation, but hopes she will have an enjoyable day.*' I couldn't stop Violet if she were determined to try it, and my short acquaintance with her suggested that she was a very determined woman, but there must be some way of letting her know that she couldn't rely on my help. The evening trip to the water tanks seemed to be my best chance. All it needed was a touch of the hand, a shake of the head. She'd be angry, of course, but at least she should have the sense to keep quiet.

I lay down and waited until evening, trying to make

myself relax and save energy. But when the stampings and clankings along the corridor began I was still as fidgety as a cat on a windy night.

There was something wrong too. The sounds were coming from the far end of the corridor, the high numbers, working down. This wasn't unusual in itself. They sometimes did vary the routine a little, and anyway the rotas would be all over the place for coronation leave.

'Out you come, number five.'

It was as much as I could do not to bound out, not to look at the locked door of cell number two as I passed. I lingered as long as I could in the lavatory cubicle, made a long job of refilling my water pail, but it was no use. No Violet. Infuriatingly, one wardress was just about to unlock her door as another one took me back. So I had to rely on the water pipe after all. That night, the place was unusually restless, with a babble of wordless messages circulating, tapped on pipes, on walls, even from ceilings to the floor above. Some of the excitement and party mood of the world outside had filtered into the prison in that peculiar way that it does, bringing not celebration but restlessness. At least it meant my message to Violet wouldn't stand out. I tapped out her number and mine then, several times, the morse code for 'No'. Whether Violet understood morse or not I'd no idea, but it was a case of trying anything. Then I tried again, this time with a simple, regular beat that I hoped might signify a passing of monotonous days, trying to reverse the urgency of her messages to me. It was useless. That night Violet, the great communicator, wouldn't answer at all. That, more than anything else, showed me how serious she was about the attempt.

So I started on a new cycle of worries. Could I let her try whatever it was without me and get herself into bad trouble? Was it my duty to her to try to stop her, not by telling the wardresses, of course, but in some other way? The one certain thing seemed to be that the coming day would bring some kind of crisis and I must be ready to react. Sleep might have been a good precaution, but it was no use trying. I unrolled my bedding and lay down on the planks in case anybody looked through the spy-hole, but I was still wide awake when the thick glass in the window turned slowly from dark to yellowish-white. Around four o'clock, probably. Out in the streets around Buckingham Palace and Westminster the early risers would already be taking up their places, with flags and sandwiches and bottles of drink. Men would be sleeking the carriage horses in the Royal Mews, polishing belt buckles at Knightsbridge Barracks. I wondered suddenly how the lion and unicorn would be spending the day.

Breakfast, tea and porridge, as usual. Roll up bedding, wash and polish mug, plate and pail also as usual. 'They shall keep their cells, utensils, clothing and bedding clean and neatly arranged' – rule number eight for the Conduct of Convicted Criminal Prisoners. Nothing in those rules about not trying to escape, but don't build on it. Inspection, also as usual except that the senior wardress had her hair done more elaborately than usual. Lunch, two slices of cold fat beef instead of one to mark the auspicious day. God save King George. Wonder if he'd like my share of the beef. Lunch must mean it was afternoon now. She'd said, 'Could be any time, but afternoon probably.'

Footsteps along the corridor, a door opening, then another. More footsteps, then a key in my door.

'Hurry up, number five, work to do.'

Misery Minny herself, stone-faced. My heart lurched. After the first glance I didn't look at her, but walked past her into the corridor. There were three more prisoners waiting there, under the care of a younger, sulky-looking wardress. Two of them I didn't recognise. The third was turned away from me, towards the stairs, but even from her thin, tense back I recognised her as Violet. There was no chance to talk to her because at once we were moved off down the stairs, the younger wardress first, then Violet followed by the other two prisoners, then me with Misery Minny bringing up the rear. We went out into the thin sunshine, with a small breeze blowing, around the exercise yard where there were other women trudging in a circle, along a path between two blocks. All the time Violet walked with her head down, hands clenched at her sides. I had an idea that we were heading for the back gate, which turned out to be the case. We came to a yard with a Black Maria parked in it alongside a baker's motor wagon. The back of the baker's wagon was open and the baker and his assistant were unloading trays of sticky buns. The number of coronation treats for the prisoners was getting downright outrageous. At this rate there'd be questions in Parliament. I looked at the back gates. They were at least twelve feet high with revolving spikes on the top. Beside the gates was a square, single storey building in harsh new brick, clearly a recent addition to the prison. There was a chimney to one side of it letting out wafts of steam. One of the prisoners in front of me murmured, 'Laundry duties.'

So far I hadn't worked in the laundry block, although it's one of the main industries of Holloway. We take in washing from the men's prisons as well as doing our own. Misery Minny knocked on a side door and our party were admitted into a concrete-floored barn of a room with wooden partitions round it, like horse stalls. A party of prisoners were already at work under the supervision of several wardresses sorting bed clothes into the stalls, ready for boiling. There was a smell of ammonia and cheap soap. The air was so hot and clammy from the coppers steaming away in an adjoining room that you started perspiring as soon as you walked in. Two of our party were told to join the women doing the sorting and the younger wardress stayed with them. That left just Violet and myself under the care of Misery Minny. She looked at us and jerked her head towards a corridor leading off the sorting room. Violet, head down, followed and I fell into line behind her. I knew now that we must be near Violet's escape point, which meant the wardress was an accomplice. If I said anything with the other wardresses only a shout away it would mean disaster for both of them.

A door opened off the corridor, no lock on it, into another and smaller sorting room. This one had a bad smell about it, only partially masked by disinfectant, and there were wicker hampers and piles of men's vests and drawers on the floor. A tank and a wooden pole stood in the corner of the room.

'You wait there.'

Misery Minny's voice was harsh with strain. She didn't look at us. Violet shifted towards me so that her arm was against mine. Even through two layers of sleeve I could feel the blood thumping through it, as desperate as the drumming on the pipe had been. Nothing I could say would stop her. Misery Minny went to a big cupboard in the corner. There was a key on the outside of the cupboard lock and the door opened into a kind of a larder with a step going down. It was stacked with carboys and bottles of disinfectant. Minny pushed the door open, stepped down with her back to us. Quick as soap sliding, Violet grabbed the wooden pole from beside the tank and hit her on the back of the head with it. Misery Minny gave a gasp and slipped down tidily onto her knees, head on a shelf beside the bottles. Violet slammed the cupboard door on her and turned the key.

'Come on, Nell.'

The decision I made there and then wasn't the one I'd worked out in the early hours of the morning. I glanced at the locked cupboard door, at Violet standing white-faced, with the key in her hand.

'Well done,' I said.

NINE

I KNEW MISERY MINNY COULDN'T be seriously hurt. Violet hadn't hit her hard enough for that and she'd gone down too neatly. There was plenty of air in the cupboard, more than enough to last until the other wardresses missed us and came to see what was wrong. She'd have a story ready by then, how we'd set upon her, coshed her and thrown her into the disinfectant store.

How *we* had, that was the point. Even if I had decided to play the good prisoner, to stay there and tell the story of how Violet had escaped, nobody would believe me. If Misery Minny broke down and admitted what she'd done my case would have been even worse, as I had a pretty firm idea by now of the part my grandmother's gold watch had played in Violet's plot. I was firmly implicated either in a violent escape attempt from Holloway or bribing a wardress. Just what you'd expect from an anarchist who tries to dynamite Scotland Yard. In the circumstances although escape still didn't look like a good idea, waiting around was an even worse one.

'What's next?'

Violet seemed temporarily speechless with the nervous effort, but her mind was still working. She pointed to a heap of dark blue in a corner. Wardresses' uniforms awaiting washing, much stained. Without another word we were stripping off our aprons and green skirts and blouses, scrabbling among the pile of blue. In a few seconds we'd got into dresses and were helping each other, fumble-fingered, with buttons. I kept glancing towards the locked cupboard,

77

but there was no sound from inside. Whatever arrangement Violet had made with Misery Minny must have included a margin of time before she started shouting. We were listening all the time in case anybody came from the big sorting room, but the only sound was men's voices from out in the yard.

'What about the caps?'

Wardresses wore smart caps like nurses, but black. There were none of those visible, so we stripped off our white prisoners' bonnets and went bare-headed. We looked at each other and I saw in Violet's eyes a stunned expression, as if she couldn't believe that we were really doing this. I expect mine was the same. Apart from that, we looked reasonably convincing wardresses, though a little stained and ruffled.

'How are we supposed to get out?'

Violet swallowed hard.

'There's some wardresses being let out early at four o'clock, for the street parties. We hide behind the empty hampers round the back until we see them coming out, then we tag on.'

We'd no way of knowing how long it was until four o'clock, but I thought it might be as much as two hours. Surely Misery Minny wouldn't stay undiscovered for that long.

'She says the door to the unloading bay's open.'

With a last glance at the locked door I went to check the corridor. Empty. I nodded to Violet and we turned away from the main sorting room towards a door at the end. It was open as promised and led out to a covered concrete ramp at the back of the laundry block. Empty wicker hampers were stacked against the wall. The first place any search party would look. I began to wonder if the whole thing were a trap.

'You stay there, Violet. I'm going to look round the corner.'

She didn't want to be left but I gave her no choice. Walking as normally as possible, as if I had a right to be

78

there, I turned the corner from the loading bay into the
yard. It was just as we'd seen it a few minutes before, with
an empty Black Maria and the baker's van unloading buns.
There were only a few trays to go now. I walked quickly back
to the pile of hampers.

'All right, we're not waiting for the wardresses. We'll
drive out.'

She gave me an alarmed look.

'How?'

'We walk up to the baker, tell him we've been allowed off
duty early, so how about a lift into town to see some of the
celebrations.'

If this were a plot and Violet were part of it, she'd object to
this change of plan. I saw her hesitate, then she nodded. We
walked together to the yard. She hurried and I didn't try to
stop her. It would make it more convincing. The baker and
his assistant were just strolling back with the air of a job well
done. We lingered by the cab of the lorry. The baker was a
plump man, with thinning hair carefully combed across a
bald head.

'Any room for two?' I said.

He smiled doubtfully.

'We've just come off duty. If we hurry we might catch the
tail-end of the procession coming back.'

'Well ladies, you know I'm not supposed to . . .'

Violet leaned against the lorry cab and put her foot
playfully on the running board.

'Aw, go on, be a sport! Don't we deserve a bit of fun like
everyone else?'

I think she'd intended to give him an encouraging flash
of ankle, only the effect was spoiled by thick stocking and
prison shoe. She took her foot off the running board hastily,
but the invitation she'd managed to put into her voice did
the trick. He began to smile.

'It's not something you get every day, is it? The king being
crowned, I mean.'

He gave in.

'All right ladies, only you'll have to go in the back and

don't tell anyone I let you. Highbury underground station do you?'

Do fine, we assured him, and clambered into a space smelling of sweet bun glaze and warm dough. His grinning assistant shut the doors on us then we heard the sound of the engine being cranked. We looked at each other but didn't dare speak. The engine came to life, the van shuddered and began to move. It soon stopped for a check at the back gate. It was probably the duty of the guard there to look inside, but I was relying on the familiarity of the baker's van and the half-heartedness of a guard who had to work while most of London was on holiday. Not much to count on, but the best we had.

'Here, is that all we're getting?'

A complaining voice from outside the van. Then the baker's voice, echoing from inside.

'No cream horns today, too busy, but we've put you in extra doughnuts.'

The guard started to say something about not forgetting the cream horns on Monday, the baker laughed and we were moving again. Down the short hill into the Holloway Road. I knew every foot of it the way you do know a place when it's your first sight of freedom after months in prison, and although I couldn't see it this time, I could imagine it. We sat perched on the empty racks where the bun trays had been, hardly daring to breathe.

Once we'd turned into Holloway Road itself, progress was slow and noisy. I risked a glance out of the small back window and saw that all the parties from the side streets were spilling out onto the main road, almost blocking it. A pub on the corner looked as if it were under siege and men with pint glasses staggered into the way of the traffic. Three women in hats with red, white and blue flowers danced across the road behind us, arms round each other's shoulders. One on the end saw me looking out and waved. A policeman was trying to persuade a children's fancy dress procession to get back on the pavement, entirely without success. Somebody had thrown a streamer round his shoulders. A boy dressed as a goose was trying to peck him in the backside. From the one glance I had at his hot face, if somebody had told him there were two escaping prisoners inside the baker's van, he wouldn't have cared.

Violet had found a bun on the floor, crumpled but whole, and was eating it. She offered it to me.

'Want a bite?'

It was the first thing either of us had said since we got into the van. I took a bite and gave it back to her. I trusted her. It wasn't a plot against me so it was all right, we were simply on the run, in disguise and I was probably top of the wanted list as a dangerous anarchist. Nothing to worry about. It took a long time to travel the short distance to Highbury Station. I was glad of that because it gave me time to recover from the shock of the escape and think about what to do next. It was a surprise to find that you could be on the one hand engaged in total madness and on the other capable of more or less coherent thought, like thinking while drowning.

Madness beyond a shadow of a doubt was what it was. You didn't just drive out of Holloway. We had no money, no plans that I knew about and only the most obvious of disguises. The probability of recapture within hours was strong. We shouldn't have got even this far if it hadn't been for the general anarchy of coronation day. I'd wanted to get out of Holloway and help Simon, wanted it so much that I wondered whether I'd willed somehow Violet's whole crazy plan. But now I was out, I didn't see what I could do without dragging other people into my illegalities. The van turned a corner and the noise of street parties faded into the distance. We slowed to a crawl and stopped. I found I was oddly reluctant to leave the friendly, good-smelling van and was angry with myself. I'd got what I wanted, hadn't I? I was free. If it was only for a few hours then the only thing that made sense was to use those few hours to start what I'd been so impatient to do in the cells – follow up the small clues I had and produce something the police couldn't ignore. It was, after all, going to be a very expensive freedom so should be used for something.

'Terminus, ladies.'

The doors opened. We were parked in an alleyway at the back door of the bakery. We clambered out – taking care not to show our ankles this time – and thanked him.

'You'll have missed most of the excitement by now. Station's that way.'

We walked up the alleyway side by side towards the station. We had no money to take the train into the city centre, but to do anything else would arouse suspicion. We were already conspicuous enough in our wardresses' uniform and hatless.

'Had you thought what you were going to do?' I asked Violet.

She shook her head.

'I just wanted to get out of that place.'

'And she agreed? Just for my watch?'

'I promised you'd pay her fifty quid as well. You don't have to, of course. Nothing she can do about it.'

'How did you know? You'd only been in there for a day or two.'

'From when I was in last time, in February. You get to know. She nearly did it then for somebody else, only she didn't trust her to pay up. That's why I thought about it when I saw your watch.'

'A down payment?'

'Yes, and she said the suffragette prisoners were straight whatever else, so she knew you'd pay up in the end.'

I tried to sort out the ethical implications of that and gave up.

'Why did she want the money so much?'

'Her husband's run off with another woman so she has to support herself. Doesn't like being in Holloway and wants to go into dress-making with her sister-in-law, only she wants seventy quid for the partnership.'

'Will she get away with this?'

Violet shrugged. I sensed a depression settling on her. From the moment she'd been arrested she'd concentrated

82

all her energy on one thing, being free. Now she had it, however briefly, and reaction was setting in.

'You must have some kind of plan.'

'Get abroad. They say Paris is all right.'

'How will you get there without money?'

She gave me a sideways look.

'I can always get money.'

We reached the station and, without discussion, walked past it and turned down Canonbury Road, dodging traffic. There were more people about here and we were collecting glances. My feet were sliding around in the hopeless shoes and Violet said hers were too small and pinched.

'Where are we going?'

She seemed to take it for granted that we'd stay together.

'I'm thinking.'

Another procession came out of a side street, surging along on a wave of beer fumes and accordion music. Violet grabbed a trailing red, white and blue streamer from a child's pram as it hurtled past and twined it in her hair.

'Less conspicuous this way.'

She was right. It distracted attention from the uniform and made it look more like fancy dress. We found a discarded cardboard sailor's hat in a gutter with 'HMS George' in gold letters round the brim. When I let my hair down and pinned it on at an angle she said you'd never guess we hadn't been out on the razzle all day. Limping and arm in arm, probably looking as drunk as any pair in the whole of celebrating London, we went our slow way.

TEN

BY THE TIME WE GOT to King's Cross, bobbing in the wake of various street parties like corks on a choppy sea, I'd got my ideas into some kind of order.

'What I need is a political hostess.'

Violet gave me a look.

'What I need is a pint of shandy.'

Not just any political hostess. It had to be one who'd know about the Withering family. If I stood even a slim chance of finding out why Robert Withering was shot, I needed to know more about him. In particular, I needed to confirm my suspicion that he had either been working for the police or engaged in some campaign of his own.

'She'll have to be a Liberal, of course.'

'As liberal as you like, as far as I'm concerned.'

Violet wasn't taking much notice of what I was saying. She ran a finger round the inside of her heel and winced, looking longingly at a motor bus as it rattled past us on its way west, crammed with celebrating people.

'Wish we were on it.'

Since my plan would involve going westward to the fashionable area I was about to say it was a good idea, until I remembered that we hadn't a halfpenny between us.

'Odd to think we can't even afford to get on a bus.'

'That never happened to you before?'

I looked at the expression on her face, genuinely questioning, and felt ashamed. I thought I'd been poor from time to time and I certainly wasn't rich now. I knew what it was to live in Paris on a few francs a day. Still,

I'd never in my life till now been destitute to the point where I'd be thrown off a bus.

'Violet, I'm not good for you. I'm going to do something this evening that will probably get me arrested again. I don't want to drag you into it.'

'What are you going to do?'

'There is a friend who might tell me something I want to know, but she lives in Mayfair. Mayfair will be full of policemen and you and I will stand out like . . .'

'Like flies in a bowl of white soup. You don't have to tell me. Well, why not? We might as well be in Mayfair as anywhere else. There's a place I know used to be quite a good pitch if you . . .'

'We're not looking for a pitch. Imagine if you got picked up by the police again.'

'Yes, and I'm not dressed for it anyway, am I?'

These two considerations worked better than any argument about morality. We walked westward along the Euston Road, beside a slow moving stream of motor- and horse-drawn traffic, mostly heading in the same direction. The air was full of horns hooting and cab drivers shouting at each other. It was just past eight by the station clock and the party mood of coronation day was extending into the long summer evening. By now it had acquired a certain doggedness, as if all concerned were determined to make the celebrations last as long as possible before subsiding back into working life. We passed men and women, sitting on the kerb with their feet in the gutter, clutching bottles. Several offered us drinks, but unfortunately their bottles were empty.

In the part of London for which we were heading, the statesmen and peers who'd taken part in the coronation ceremonies would be bathing and changing into their evening finery for a round of dinners and balls. I was certain that my friend Geraldine would be giving a party and that was where we were heading. Acquaintance rather than friend, perhaps. I liked her, but didn't know her well enough to guess how she'd stand up to the shock I was about to inflict. She was a sympathiser with our cause, but hadn't yet managed to kick off the family shackles to the point of joining us. I had to admit that in her case the shackles were heavy as well as gold plated. Her grandfather and her father were both distinguished politicians in the Liberal Party, one in the Lords and the other in the Commons. Geraldine was married to a stupefyingly dull barrister but because her father was a widower, she also acted as his hostess on grand occasions. She lived at the centre of Liberal politics, which meant ruling party politics, and if anybody could tell me about the Witherings, Geraldine could.

We passed several policemen on our way to Mayfair without attracting a second glance. They all looked tired to death.

'You know,' Violet said, 'this isn't such a bad idea. They wouldn't expect us to make for a place like this.'

In spite of her tiredness and sore feet she was brightening at the sight of the carriages, of men in evening suits and women in silks and cascades of jewels going up the steps to houses with windows blazing with lights and the sound of waltzes coming from inside. She even danced a few steps along the pavement until she noticed another policeman on the corner.

'Is it far from here?'

'Not far.'

Geraldine's family house took up most of one side of a small square and looked as if it were hosting one of the grandest parties of all. Carriages were queueing up round three sides of the square and women in pastel-coloured dresses pressed against each other up the steps like sweet peas jammed into a vase. I led the way round to the back entrance. As I'd hoped, this was the same picture of confusion, but less decorous. Although the party could hardly have started, reinforcements of champagne and food were already being called in. The wine merchant's man was arguing with somebody over a crate of broken eggs. The iceman's boy was trying to push his way through with an immense cube of ice dripping from giant tongs. I lurked with Violet by the railings until the ice slipped out of the tongs and they were nearly coming to blows then, when everybody was distracted by the argument, we dashed down the basement steps and into the steaming civil war of the scullery region. There were so many other people coming and going in such a state of industrious panic that nobody even glanced at us.

We stood and looked at each other beside tables loaded with rose and apricot coloured sorbets stretching away into the distance like pack-ice.

'Don't just stand there. All washers-up wanted in the scullery.'

This from a man in a white jacket as he dodged round us. Naturally he'd taken us for washers-up, the lowest creatures in the hierarchy. We found long white aprons with bibs hanging up behind the scullery door as we went in and hastily tied them on. The scullery was in the grip of its own panic because the butler had rejected several trays of champagne glasses after spotting a greasy thumb print on one of them, so they all had to be washed and dried as the guests were arriving. Violet and I were virtually seized by the scruffs of our necks and flung into the action at a row of deep stoneware sinks.

It was an hour at least before we could draw breath again, and by then Violet looked like a half-drowned kitten. The first of the used plates and glasses from upstairs were beginning to come down to us, but at this early stage of the party it was no more than a trickle. A few of the women lit cigarettes and began to chat among themselves. I had time to wonder how I could make my way up from the nether regions to the glittering summit of all this where Geraldine would be presiding.

'Dustpan and brush. Dustpan and brush wanted in the drawing room.'

The cry went up. I dived under the sink, found what was wanted and dashed for the door. The next room was one of the kitchens and the men and women in their white jackets and aprons drew away from my uncleanness as

I shot through. Beyond the kitchen was a flight of stairs going up then a short corridor leading to a green baize door. I knew as well as anybody that the green baize door was a barrier through which the likes of washing-up women never passed. On the other side of it were the Quality, along with such clean and well-drilled servants as might breathe the same air. They were the sleek duck's back, we the duck's legs paddling away frantically below the water line to keep things moving. A maid would be waiting on the other side of the door, properly clothed in black dress, white cuffs and apron or possibly, since this was a grand occasion, even a footman. She or he would take the dustpan and brush from me, hurry to the drawing room to brush up the broken glass or crushed tartlet, then deliver the remains to me for disposal as I waited on the dirty side of the door. That was the procedure, only tonight it couldn't be allowed to happen that way.

As I approached the door I started walking faster, building up momentum. When I got to it I flung it open and walked straight through without slowing down, holding dustpan and brush in front of me like a passport. It was a maid waiting, a young one, with her hand held out ready. As I marched past her she fell back, open-mouthed, too stunned by this breach of protocol to say or do anything. I was on the ground floor. The butler, letting in late arrivals, had his back to me. I strode on upstairs, dodging past chatting couples, to a huge first floor landing, all mirrors and lilies. So far nobody had tried to stop me or even noticed me. There was a half-open doorway on the left and I swerved into it, ready to say if challenged that I'd come to sweep up the glass, ma'am. Mercifully it was a small lounge, empty of people. It looked as if it had been set aside for ladies to come and relax in the intervals from dancing, but so far nobody was tired. I put down my dustpan and brush and swooped on a prize lying to hand on a little pie-crust table, a ball card in ivory parchment paper with a gold tassel and little silver pencil attached, all ready to keep a record of what dances were promised to what gentlemen. No entries in it yet, but I soon dealt with that.

'*Geraldine, Please meet me by the jasmine in the conservatory as soon as possible. I am in trouble and need your help.*'

I signed it riskily with my full name, since there was no certainty she'd recognise my writing, and wrote her name on the back.

All that remained now was to get it delivered. I waited until the landing was clear then slipped out and lurked behind a marble statue of Hermes, surrounded by greenery and white lilies. A group of people came chatting up the stairs. A footman hovered with a tray of champagne. They'd all of them perfected the art of getting their hands round a glass of champagne without even appearing to notice it was there. As they moved on I flipped the ball card onto the tray among the glasses. The poor man goggled at me in a way that would have got him the part of frog footman in any pantomime in the country. From among the greenery I gave him the best I could manage in the way of haughty glares. He looked from me to the ball card on the tray and back again.

'Deliver it at once, if you'd be so kind.'

I borrowed the tone of voice from my least favourite aunt, but it worked like a charm. He gave me another disbelieving glance then hurried off with a bobbing walk, almost a run. So far, so good.

I'd never set foot in Geraldine's house before. Although it had been an easy assumption that there would be a conservatory, and naturally any well regulated conservatory would have jasmine in June, getting there without being thrown out was the next problem. Downstairs and off to the side was a reasonable guess for the location. I waited until I heard the butler opening the front door again to what sounded like a large group of people, then came out from behind Hermes and picked up the biggest vase of lilies I could find. Once I had my hands under it only my white apron, the lower part of my dress and the Holloway shoes were showing. My face and the upper part of my body must have been quite hidden by the flowers and foliage and my view through them was approximately that of a caterpillar in a herbaceous border. When I'd got a firm grip on the vase I advanced downstairs as confidently as I could, just as the latest arrivals were coming up. Through my petals I glimpsed an evening shirt with pearl studs, a neck with an emerald collar. One of the women gave a little exclamation of surprise as they stood aside for me, but then if the hostess chooses to have the floral arrangements moved around after the party has begun, it would be ill bred in a guest to comment.

At the bottom of the stairs a footman advanced. I said, in what I hoped was a housekeeperly voice, that some of the lilies were wilting. There were replacements in the conservatory, if he would be kind enough to open doors for me. The blessed man did exactly as I asked, no arguing. A door to the right, a door to the left, a long expanse of soft carpet that was the kindest thing my feet had walked on for a long time, then he opened a high glass door and there I was in paradise, or at least the nearest equivalent to it in Mayfair, with the scent of jasmine curling itself round me like the arms of a long-lost sister. The footman offered to take the vase from me. No thank you, I said, and waited until he'd gone before lowering it carefully to the floor.

There were couples in the conservatory, which was only to be expected, but they were all too occupied with each other to take any notice of me. The jasmine was trained all over an indoor bower, shading a wrought iron bench patterned with fern leaves. There was a space a few feet wide between the back of the bower and a whitewashed wall. I inserted myself into it and waited. I had to wait a long time and was the unwilling eavesdropper on several conversations. To my great embarrassment one young man was obviously trying to work up courage to propose to the lovely girl sitting beside him. I was seriously considering whether I ought not to move at any risk, until she unknowingly saved me by saying it really was terribly hot and could he possibly get her another glass of fruit cup? He went and before he could get back she went too. Soon after that, Geraldine arrived at last.

There's a line in Tennyson somewhere about a woman being in gloss of satin and glimmer of pearls. Geraldine looked like that, all gloss and glimmer, with orchids spilling over one bare shoulder, the family tiara half hidden in her fair hair. But she arrived at as near a run as can be managed in full evening dress and stood tapping nervously at her chest with her fan, biting her lip.

'Geraldine, I'm in here.'

She gasped and came round behind the bower of jasmine as nervously as if she expected to be ambushed.

'Nell!'

Her eyes widened and her jaw dropped.

'What's happening? And why on earth are you wearing that hat?'

I'd forgotten about the sailor's hat till that moment. No wonder the frog footman had stared. I took it off, but that didn't seem to comfort her.

'For heaven's sake, what's happening? Is it some kind of demonstration?'

The idea of it horrified her. It's one thing to support a political cause, quite another if it threatens to disrupt a social event you've been planning for months. I sympathised – up to a point.

'Nothing like that. I need to know all you can tell me about Robert Withering.'

It took her some time to adjust to that. She was still trying to recover from the shock of finding me there at all.

'But . . . he's dead.'

'Yes, I know. I was there.'

Her brain was beginning to work again, the sheer panic in her eyes changing to puzzlement.

'Weren't you sent to . . .?'

'Yes. I escaped. I dare say they'll catch up with me soon, so I need to find out as much as I can before that.'

Her head sank until her chin was crushing the orchids.

She whispered, 'And the Home Secretary's drinking champagne upstairs.'

'Don't worry, I don't expect you to introduce us.' I envied him the champagne though. 'You haven't seen me. I promise not to make trouble for you, only please, please, tell me what you know about Withering.'

Her head stayed down and her eyes closed while she made her decision. When she looked up she was the poised and intelligent woman I remembered.

'What do you want to know?'

'Was he the kind of man who'd work for the police?'

'No, of course not.'

'As a spy, I mean.'

'Nell, he was a revolutionary, a communist. He nearly drove his father mad, and as for his poor mother . . .'

'How long had you known him?'

'Practically from infancy. His elder sister and I were best friends at school. I suppose he'd have been about seven when I first took any notice of him.'

'He wasn't a revolutionary then?'

'I don't know about revolutionary, but he was a holy terror even then. He was the only boy in the family and his mother spoiled him terribly. I remember when he got expelled from Eton . . .'

'What for?'

'It was when the fighting was going on in South Africa and Robert had decided to be a pro-Boer.'

'So he was expelled for his political opinions?'

'They didn't mind the political opinions. He locked his house master in the coal cellar for disagreeing with him.'

'What happened after that?'

'Well, they hushed it up, of course, and sent him to a crammer and got him into Christ Church. He was calling himself a communist by then, but nobody minded much once he was at university, and his father decided he should go into the Foreign Office.'

'As a communist?'

'They thought it was a phase he was going through.

92

Anyway, his father said he should improve his languages, so he sent him to the Continent for a year on quite a good allowance. He spent a few months in Paris, then he went off to Geneva and seems to have got into really bad company.'

'Anarchists?'

'Communists, anarchists, the lot. His father and mother went out to try to persuade him to come back and apparently it ended in the most horribly embarrassing scene. His father cut off his allowance, of course, but it wouldn't surprise me if his mother's still sending him something from time to time. Sent, I mean. Oh god.'

I held up a finger to warn her that there was somebody on the other side of the jasmine bower. The young man who'd been trying to propose was back with a glass of fruit cup, amazed to find the girl not there. He stood staring at the bench in a moon-calf way as if she might have made herself invisible and would appear again if he looked long enough. Then he walked up and down staring so fixedly at the foliage that I was worried he might see his hostess and me behind it. Geraldine was worried too and froze, looking at me with big, horrified eyes. When he eventually dragged himself away I had to prompt her to start talking again.

'When did he come back to England?'

'That's one of the worst things about it. The family didn't even know he was back in the country until a policeman came round on Saturday evening and asked his father to come and identify the body. They're devastated, of course. His father's trying to play the ancient Roman, saying Robert was no son of his, and so on. You know he hoped to be Chancellor, but even though it's not his fault it's hardly a recommendation to have a son who tried to blow up Scotland Yard, is it?'

'And his mother?'

'She just keeps on about poor Robert always getting into bad company. Which is all very well, except that the reason why Robert was always in bad company was that he was the one who made it bad.'

She was relaxing just a little, back in the world she knew, letting her fan unfurl itself the width of a butterfly's wing. But her eyes were shifting around all the time, fearing discovery with me.

'Was he a dislikeable man to meet?'

'Quite the reverse, that was the trouble.'

'Trouble?'

'You know, the Byronic thing – mad, bad and dangerous to know. There are some women who find that attractive. He could be charming and he really was quite good looking. A cousin of mine nearly got engaged to him while he was up at Oxford, until my aunt very sensibly put her foot down. If he had gone into the Foreign Office, you could have imagined him ending up as ambassador to Paris.'

'Apart from being a revolutionary.'

'Apart from that.'

The conservatory door opened and a wave of waltz music came through. Geraldine fidgeted like a horse wanting to be away.

'I know, you must go. I really am very, very grateful. You never saw me. I never saw you.'

'Thank you, Nell.' She smiled a wan smile, then the reality of it hit her. 'But what are you going to do? Where are you going to go?'

'Better not ask me.'

'Is . . . is there anything I can do?'

It was brave, because she was terrified I might take her up on it.

'You've done it already.'

Even if everything she'd told me had demolished the only theory that had made sense to me so far. If Withering had been a police spy, then he'd been preparing his false identity whole-heartedly from about the age of sixteen, which was so obviously out of the question that I had to abandon the idea. But in that case, why were the police behaving so oddly?

'There is just one thing, Geraldine, if you could manage it . . .'

The relief on her face faded.

'What?'

'I hate to ask this, but I am literally penniless for the moment. If you could . . .'

I'd seldom felt so embarrassed.

'Of course. Would . . .?'

She looked around for her bag, then her face turned as red as mine felt. Of course a woman at her own ball doesn't carry coins and notes around.

'Sorry, Geraldine. Silly of me. It really doesn't matter. You'd better go now, while the coast is clear.'

She grabbed my hand and squeezed it then slipped out from our hiding place and back into society. I felt sorry for what I'd done to her, and grateful. She'd done almost all a friend could be expected to do in the circumstances. I couldn't have asked for more.

ELEVEN

GETTING BACK TO THE SCULLERY was easier than escaping from it. I simply gave Geraldine two minutes' start then strode to the green baize door, past little groups of guests who decided I was one of those regrettable incidents that must be ignored. I found Violet surprisingly cheerful. She'd made friends with some of the other washing-up women and they were competing for the substantial scraps of food that came down on the used plates.

'What have you been doing then, Nell?' She waved an asparagus spear at me then engulfed it neatly, tip first. 'You can have the next one. Fixed up beds for us then, have you?'

'Not quite.'

I joined her at the sink, plunging my hands into soapy water and grabbing a passing plate to look convincing. It was clear that the ball would go on into the early hours, probably until dawn. My original idea had been that Violet and I would leave as soon as I'd had my talk with Geraldine, but I was revising it. Walking the streets of the West End in the early hours would be a sure way to get arrested again, not to speak of the temptations for Violet. And surely one place the police wouldn't think of looking for two escaped prisoners was the scullery of a government minister, with the Home Secretary visiting upstairs.

'I thought we might stay here washing up all night.'

'Yes. The others have been hired until seven in the morning, or whenever we've finished doing the breakfast things. Ten bob for twelve hours, and it gets quieter round about two o'clock, so you can have a kip in a corner somewhere.'

So that settled it. Soon afterwards boys arrived and heaved trayfuls of dirty plates into the sinks, and the next few hours were a chaos of suds and slithery things, avalanches of plates and cutlery at unpredictable intervals and trying desperately to keep awake, keep scrubbing, and not pitch forward from sheer tiredness into the grey and swirling water. Violet must have felt as bad, and yet she kept up a stream of chatter with the women on either side of us and her occasional shriek of laughter rang out over the clashing of china and the shouts and arguments from the kitchen next door.

Sometime in the early hours the pace slackened as predicted. I have a dim memory of eating the remains of salmon en croûte while somebody mopped the floor round me, then curling up with others on damp flour sacks under the scullery table and plunging at once into a sleep as deep as hibernating underground.

I was dragged out of it around dawn by a clamour that made me think the police had arrived, but it turned out to be a crisis caused by the lack of clean forks for breakfast. It was followed by the discovery of a cache of unwashed forks in a sink, recrimination and protest, hasty washing of guilty forks with waiters standing over and fidgeting like sprinters at the starting line, and the delivery of bacon and eggs to people who'd been dancing all night. While this was going on I took Violet to one side.

'We'd better go.'

There would be people on the streets outside by now, milkmen and delivery boys, enough for us not to be conspicuous.

'We don't get paid till after seven.'

We could do with the money. A pound between us would transform things, and heaven knows we'd earned it.

'I don't think we can wait. The housekeeper's bound to have a list of people they hired and if she finds two extra she'll ask questions.'

I didn't want to be caught. I didn't want to embarrass Geraldine any more either. Violet was reluctant, but saw the point. We walked out of the back door and up the steps from the basement, still with our white aprons on. At least they helped to hide the wardresses' uniforms to some extent, but we were still a sight, dishevelled and hatless. Violet was limping from blisters and I could see that the rise in spirits that had come from being with the other women was fading fast.

'Where are we going now?'

'Another friend.'

'Another rich one?'

'Anything but.'

I'd had time to think while washing the forks. Geraldine had helped me as much as she could, but what I knew now about Withering had put me back rather than forward. The only thing to do now was to try tackling it from the other side, the anarchist side. There was one friend of mine who knew a lot about revolutionary groups without being a member of one himself as far as I knew. I took us back eastwards, by way of Piccadilly, Shaftesbury Avenue and Holborn, through streets scattered with empty bottles and torn streamers. London was waking up slowly and reluctantly that morning after coronation day. We saw only two policemen on the whole journey, and they didn't give us a second glance.

There's a little low building in a street a few hundred yards from Liverpool Street station that vibrates almost constantly to the sound of trains as they begin to get up steam for the journey eastwards. It used to be a meeting place for Bible classes. What goes on there now is secular but almost as devotional. It's where people meet to play chess. The name outside it, in neat white letters on a blue board, is the Archimedes J. Stuggs Chess Forum, after a man who made his money in the catering trade and left all of it in his will 'for the encouragement of the intellectually ennobling pursuit of chess among the working classes', to the considerable annoyance of his family.

Violet studied the notice, hot and dusty, shifting from one blistered foot to the other.

'Is this what we've come all this way for?'

'I hope so, if my friend's there.'

The friend, Max Blume, was a journalist active in various good causes, at that time editor of a small magazine advocating an end to meat-eating and the burning of coal as a solution to war, greed and sinus trouble. But the enthusiasm he gave to these causes was mere dilettanteism compared to his passion for chess. Quite what it is that draws people on the left of politics towards chess I don't know. On one occasion when I'd visited the club I'd seen a man who was wanted by the police in both Paris and London intent on a game with a respectable university professor and nobody at all concerned about it. Even more to the point, it had become a social gathering place for exiles from Russia and the Baltic states who'd found asylum here from the activities of the political police at home.

We limped past the dustbins to a church-like door under a corrugated iron porch and lifted the latch. Inside it was just as on any other day, a large bare room with a tea urn on a trestle table by the door, smaller tables dotted around the bare floorboards, dust motes suspended in the sun beams that threaded the stone pillars of the curtainless windows and faded the mural of Jesus teaching the children on the opposite wall. Although it was not yet ten o'clock in the morning there were at least twenty people in the room, all men. I guessed that some of them had been playing all night. A few were sitting on chairs against the wall, reading newspapers, but most were seated in pairs at the small tables, or standing watching the players. Only a few people looked up as we came in, then only in a casual and uninvolved way. Two shop-worn Bacchantes were nothing to the Archimedes J. Stuggs Chess Forum.

Max was there, luckily only watching a game, not playing, or we might have had to wait all day. I told Violet to stay by the tea urn, went up to him and touched his elbow.

'Hello, Max. Could we have a word?'

It took him a moment to tear his attention away from the game and realise who it was. His reaction was much the same as Geraldine's.

'Nell Bray. Is something wrong?'

'Quite a lot.'

I must have been looking almost as desperate as I felt, because he walked away from the game without a backward glance and followed me to the tea urn.

'This is Violet. You never saw us.'

As a journalist, he must have known something about the events on Saturday evening, including the fact that I'd been sent to prison, but he gave no sign of it. Chess has its uses.

'I'm trying to find out who tried to blow up Scotland Yard on Saturday evening.'

Chess has its limits too. His eyes widened and he rocked back on his feet.

'Hadn't you heard about it?'

His reaction was interesting. Geraldine, with direct access to the Home Secretary, had known about the attempt and spoken as if it were common knowledge among her circle.

'No. I knew about Withering being shot and Frater being arrested for it. I've been trying to find out what's going on but . . . Are you sure?'

We were having to talk in whispers, but even so we were getting glances from the chess tables. Max's shock was genuine, and he was a man who knew more about what was going on than most. The police were keeping the story of the cart loaded with dynamite to themselves, and some of the politicians. It might have been because they didn't want to cause panic in the lead-up to the coronation but after my interviews with Brust I thought it was more than that.

'You knew about Withering?'

'Yes. That's been in the papers. Shooting on Westminster Bridge and a man charged. I couldn't make any sense of it from what I knew, but if he was trying to blow up Scotland Yard . . .'

I told him the whole story, as best I could, only leaving

Geraldine's name out of it. Violet listened with an anxious expression. Some of this was new to her.

'You see, with Robert Withering's background, the only thing that seemed to make sense was that he was acting as a spy for the police, or even an agent provocateur. I thought for some reason they wouldn't admit that, so they were trying to gain time by holding poor Simon instead. I'm not so sure about that now.'

Max shook his head.

'No, if young Withering were an agent provocateur, he'd have been doing it for far too long to be credible. I've known about Withering among the anarchist groups for a couple of years. He's the real thing – as far as any bourgeois turned revolutionary is the real thing. I gather he met some Bakuninites in France or Switzerland and got converted from communism to anarchism.'

'But one of the other people on the cart shot him, I'm quite sure of that.'

'Probably some kind of internal feud. Some of the Bakuninites tend to be a bloodthirsty and bad tempered lot, and it's easy to accuse anybody of being a police spy.'

'So why are the police still holding poor Simon? I can see he might have been an obvious suspect at first but they should know how harmless he is by now. Why are they behaving so oddly?'

'Oddly? It sounds quite normal to me.'

In the past I'd always considered Max irrationally suspicious on the subject of the police and had put it down to the company he kept. I wasn't so sure now.

When I didn't reply he looked at the two of us and seemed to take in the situation for the first time.

'You were in Holloway and now you've . . .'

'Yes, Max.'

'Nell, is this wise?'

The sorrowful way he was looking at me, like a chess problem that wouldn't be solved, made me lose my temper, quite unfairly.

'No, it isn't wise. I helped get Simon arrested. That wasn't wise either. I'm on the run from Holloway, and God knows how many years I'll be in for when they catch up with me. So what do you suggest I do?'

'I . . . I could hide you for a day or two until we could get you both abroad or . . .'

This generosity in the face of my bad temper made me ashamed.

'And end up in prison yourself? No, the best thing you can do to help me is tell me if you have any idea which group was responsible.'

'If I can, I will. But at the moment I simply don't know. At least sit down and let me get you some tea.'

There was a little office to one side of the hall. He sat us down in there and brought black tea from the urn in glasses, with slices of lemon. Violet made a face at hers but drank. Max watched us and twisted his fingers together, as he does when thinking hard.

'All the Sidney Street lot are dead or on the run, besides they weren't that ambitious. There's Malatesta, but I'm nearly certain this wouldn't be his kind of thing.'

'Is there any Russian anarchist from an aristocratic background in the country, apart from Prince Kropotkin, that is?'

We all knew about Kropotkin, firmly anarchist in theory but altruistic and law-abiding in practice. He even dropped in at the Chess Forum occasionally. As a suspect for trying to blow up Scotland Yard he was about as likely as the Archbishop of Canterbury.

'What makes you think it's a Russian aristocrat?'

'A pattern on a sheet. Have you got a piece of paper?'

He gave me the margin of a discarded newspaper and the stub of a pencil. I cleared glasses aside and drew the pattern on the blue-dyed sheet and the initials as far as I could remember them.

'Well yes, it looks like Russian. Where does it come from?'

I told him.

'There's a young man who comes in here around midday,

102

one of the refugees from the Czar's secret police. Stefan, he calls himself. I'll try it on him, if you like. Can you wait?'

We could wait, I said. It was blissful to be sitting down. Max went out and came back with a plate of sandwiches, beef on rye bread. When we'd finished them and more glasses of tea Violet leaned her head back against the wall and slept.

Max came in later and went on tiptoe when he saw her. 'Will we wake her?'

I said I didn't think so, but we talked in whispers anyway.

'What worries me, Nell, is what you intend to do even if you manage to find out who's responsible. You can't pick a man or woman out of a group of anarchists and march them off to the nearest police station.'

'No.'

'Are you planning to infiltrate them? Turn informer?'

'No!'

I was getting angry again, until the force of his question struck me. It was only eighteen hours or so since my unexpected escape and all my energy in that time had been bent on staying free and finding out what I could. Because, I suppose, I hadn't expected to stay free I'd made no plans beyond that.

'I don't think I could . . .' And see Simon hanged, if it came to that? 'Max, I just don't know.'

I looked down at the dusty floorboards and made myself think.

'If I could find out something, some evidence, and go back to Scotland Yard with it, perhaps I could stop whatever game it is that they're playing. If I managed to tell somebody else about it as well – you for instance – so that we could threaten to publish it, they'd at least have to let Simon go. That's all I want.'

He twisted his fingers until the bones showed white at the knuckles.

'It's a faint hope, Nell.'

'What else is there?'

103

Soon after that he went next door to see if the young Russian, Stefan, had arrived. Later they came in together. Stefan was dark haired and nervous but he had a very upright way of walking and his threadbare clothes were neat and brushed. He gave a little bow to me and another to Violet, still asleep. Max was holding my sketch of the pattern on the sheet.

'Stefan recognises it. Have you heard of a princess Sophia?'

'No.'

'Stefan says she's running a kind of a commune out on the far side of Hampstead Heath in Muswell Hill. I thought she was settled in Geneva, but apparently she had to get out of there after some business about a man killing himself in her villa.'

Stefan listened and nodded. He obviously preferred to do his talking through Max. I sat up at the mention of Geneva. According to Geraldine's information that was where Withering had fallen more deeply into bad company.

'Is the Princess Sophia an anarchist?'

'She doesn't belong with any of the usual groups. I suppose you might describe her as an anarchist of a kind.'

'What's her background?'

'Usual wealthy and aristocratic Russian family, Stefan says. The reforming phase started with her father. He was one of the first to liberate his serfs, friend of Tolstoy and so on. Then one of his brothers wrote a pamphlet criticising some of his superior officers in the army and got shut up in the Peter and Paul fortress, so another brother tried to challenge his general to a duel and was shot for mutiny. After that they all had to leave Russia.'

I looked at Max, wondering how much he'd told Stefan.

'Would you say she was the kind of anarchist who tries to blow up things or shoot people?'

Stefan turned red and shook his head vehemently.

'She's a good woman. A little silly, perhaps, but a good woman.'

I suppose it depended what you meant by silly. By good either, come to that. I looked at Max.

'Do you know exactly where in Muswell Hill?'

'Stefan does.'

'Would he take us there?'

I thought at first that Stefan was going to refuse because it was some time before he said anything.

'You can see her nearer than that. She's in Stepney this afternoon, giving a party.'

'A party!'

Violet woke up, blinking.

'Another bloody party? I'll say this for you Nell, you do see life.'

She smiled at Stefan and he turned a deeper shade of red.

'For the children, a free people's party, instead of a coronation party.'

'Shouldn't that have been yesterday?'

'She couldn't, because all the children were at coronation parties.'

It made sense of a kind, I suppose. I asked if he'd take us there and introduce us to the princess. He glanced at Max for guidance and then said yes.

Max took me aside.

'Are you sure this is what you want to do, Nell?'

'I don't think I have much choice.'

Geneva and a pattern on a sheet weren't much in the way of clues, but they were all I had.

'How are you off for the money?'

'Nothing.'

He dug deep in his pockets and produced two half crowns, a shilling and threepence halfpenny. I took it gratefully, knowing that from the usual state of Max's finances it meant no lunch or dinner for him.

'Thanks, Max. I'll keep in touch if I can.'

'Be careful, Nell.'

I turned as we were on the pavement following Stefan to the tram stop. Max was standing in the doorway, hand raised, like an atheist trying to give a blessing. Kind of him.

TWELVE

WITH MONEY IN OUR POCKETS we had the luxury of a tram ride to Stepney. Stefan, moving like a man who knew the area, led the way from the tram stop along narrow streets, still hung with red, white and blue bunting. If Princess Sophia wanted somewhere to practise philanthropy or preach revolution this part of the East End would do as well as anywhere, full of overcrowded houses and sweatshops, and the narrow windows of grocers selling sugar by the quarter pound and tea by the half ounce. It struck me that there were fewer children around the streets than usual, but the reason became obvious when Stefan led us round a corner and came suddenly to a halt. They were all at the princess's party.

The street seethed with children, playing marbles in the gutters, chasing each other in and out of doorways, sitting at benches down trestle tables running the length of the street. Their high shouts and chattering rose and hung like a canopy over two rival kinds of music provided, a barrel organ at one end of the street and a man with a piano accordion at the other, both playing different tunes. A few adults were visible, hurrying plates of cakes and jugs of lemonade to the tables, breaking up fights, all with the distracted look of people about to sink for the third time and stay under. But there was something else that hit me harder than the noise and the crowds: the decorations. The lamp posts had big panels of cardboard tied round them with fairytale pictures of children and animals, boldly painted. There were strings running between the lamp posts with flags and banners of all colours, golden stars and suns. No crowns or red, white and blue here. There was one picture of a girl and a unicorn, well painted and quite professional. The unicorn on it might have been the younger sister of the one on the dynamite cart. As I stared at it I felt Stefan touching my elbow.

'Princess Sophia's over there.'

He was pointing to the crowd round the man with the accordion. We followed him, dodging among the children. I'd been expecting, I suppose, an anarchist aristocrat to be doom-laden and dramatic. When Stefan stopped beside a small plump woman in a black dress I thought at first that she must be one of the helpers. Then I saw he was explaining something and glancing towards Violet and me. He nodded at us and we went towards them with some difficulty because the accordion player had started 'Oranges and Lemons' and the children were forming into lines across our path.

Stefan introduced us by our first names. What he might have said about us while we were making our way through the crowd, I didn't know. The princess took my hand in a soft little paw and looked up at me. She looked to be in her fifties, with a round, lined face brightened with a gash of lip rouge. It was the same colour as the embroidered red poppies on the shawl round her shoulders. Her hair, piled up in a loose bun, was glossy black, with thick strands of grey. She smelt of eau de cologne and perspiration.

'I like your decorations,' I said, 'especially the unicorn.'

She beamed, as if my remark had been nothing but a compliment.

'Poor children should see beautiful things, nothing but beautiful things.'

Her accent was strong, but French rather than Russian, not surprising given the class she came from and most of a life in exile. She looked, and sounded, about as capable of plotting to blow up Scotland Yard as my maternal grandmother. In fact, given a choice, I'd have backed my grandmother for preference.

107

'It's very like a unicorn I saw on a cart last Saturday evening.'

Her face changed immediately, not to obvious guilt or anger, but simple grief. She'd kept hold of my hand and now her grip on it tightened.

'You were there?'

I nodded, but she kept repeating the question, looking up at me with bright little dark eyes.

'Yes, I was there. One of my friends is in prison for shooting Robert Withering, but I know he didn't do it.'

Her eyes took in Stefan and Violet and came back to me. A line of children skipped past us, pushing us aside.

'Oranges and lemons, say the bells of St Clement's
I owe you five farthings, say the bells of St Martin's.'

'We must talk. Somewhere quiet, somewhere quiet.'

She had a trick of repeating a phrase while she was thinking, then erupting into sudden action. A decisive mind, I thought, if not an orderly one. She started towing me down the lines of children, dodging under the arched arms of the pair at the end, into the opening of an alleyway where cats were disputing the remains of potted meat sandwiches. Violet and Stefan watched from the other side of the lines of dancing children.

'Who is this friend of yours? How do you know he didn't shoot poor Robert?'

I told her in detail all that had happened on Saturday evening, with an edited version of what had happened afterwards. I included my two interviews with Mr Brust of the Special Branch and noticed that she nodded when I mentioned his name. The escape from Holloway delighted her so much that she actually hugged me.

'One day we shall go back together, you and I, and we shall tear that wicked place down brick by brick and let out all the poor women into the sunshine.'

A good manifesto, if impractical. I noticed that she made no mention of dynamite, although that would have speeded up the process considerably. So far I hadn't mentioned it either. Being prisoners on the run seemed to make Violet and myself members of the family and I didn't want to destroy the good will until I'd found out as much as possible.

She began to cross-question me enthusiastically about whether I knew other acquaintances of hers who'd also been in prison. In a few cases I did, which helped a lot. She'd met Sylvia Pankhurst several times and although it was clear that the two of them weren't bosom friends that too seemed to convince her that I was trustworthy. I'd expected suspicion and hostility and felt knocked off course by her apparent open-heartedness.

'And the police have arrested your friend for shooting poor Robert? Are they going to hang him?'

She asked that in conversational tones. Perhaps, given her family history, it was a matter of course.

'Quite probably, unless I can find out who really shot him before they arrest me again.'

I'd got my hand back by then, but she repossessed it and patted it comfortingly.

'They shan't arrest you. We shall hide you, and your friend.'

'It's not just a matter of hiding from the police, I have to ask questions.'

She laughed. 'Do you think the people who shot poor Robert will tell you just because you ask them?'

'Almost certainly not, but who should I be asking?'

'The police, of course.'

More children had joined the game by now and the lines were running the length of the pavement, the accordion playing louder, a child flying past with every word we spoke.

'When will you pay me? say the bells of Old Bailey
When I grow rich, say the bells of Shoreditch.'

The princess closed her eyes, pained.

109

'So young they are taught the language of the capitalists. We must write new words for such a pretty tune. You shall help me.'

She seemed to think that was quite as important as what we were talking about.

'The police didn't shoot Robert Withering unless there was a policeman on the back of your cart.'

She'd been humming the tune. That stopped her.

'They climbed on the cart and shot him? Nobody told me that.'

I took a deep breath, while registering that she'd obviously had some report about what had happened.

'No. Nobody climbed on the cart except my friend and he certainly isn't a policeman and hadn't got a gun anyway. But the shot came from there, so it must have been one of the people in costume on the cart who killed him.'

Before I'd even finished, she was shaking her head.

'No, that's what the police will say, but they're lying as they always do. Nobody on the cart would have shot poor Robert. They're all our people. They all loved him, like I did.'

There were actually tears in her eyes. I looked at her, wondering how I could get any sense out of this, wishing that the music and chanting would stop.

'Here comes a candle to light you to bed
Here comes a chopper to chop off your head
The last man's head is – OFF.'

Yells of delight as the victim was caught.

'Like our little tableau,' she said, the tears running down her cheeks. 'We were going to do it in Whitehall.'

'Do what?'

I thought, wildly, that she was going to confess to the explosives.

'Pretend to cut the king's head off, to remind everybody how the English people were once brave enough to cut off their king's head.'

110

It made, I suppose, some weird sense of the figures on the cart. Had they intended to mime the execution of a king then set off real dynamite? I was beginning to think that anything was possible with Princess Sophia. Now, with the tears still running down her cheeks, she was waving wildly at somebody on the other side of the street.

'It is Nana. She wants me to go and cut the cake. You will excuse me?'

She dabbed hastily at her face with a crumpled linen handkerchief.

'You will wait for me, you and your friend, while we give the poor children their cake. Then you will come back with me to our farm and we shall protect you from the police with our last drop of blood.'

Violet was waiting on the pavement looking tense and puzzled. Stefan, I noticed, was handing round plates of bright red jelly.

'What were you and the old woman talking about?'

She was edgy, puzzled.

'That's the princess. She runs a kind of commune. She says she'll let us stay there out of the way of the police.'

I decided to leave out the last drop of blood, but she smelt it anyway.

'Commune! Wasn't that what they had in the French Revolution?'

'Something like it.'

I was still trying to clear from my head the giddiness of the last few minutes. Whether Princess Sophia were mad, or clever, or a mixture of both I'd landed where I needed to be. The cart had originated from her commune and Withering had been a member of it – a beloved member by her account. Of course I'd accept her invitation, but Violet couldn't be dragged into it any more deeply than I'd taken her already. This had to be where our ways parted.

'I'm going with her, but you don't need to. Stepney's probably as good a place as any to go into hiding and you can have the money that Max gave us.'

'I'm coming with you, Nell.'

'They're anarchists.'

'I'm not interested in bloody politics.'

'It's dangerous.'

'She doesn't look dangerous.'

Violet nodded towards the princess, passing big platters of pink and yellow cake down the table, children yelling and laughing on either side.

'Even if she isn't, her friends are.'

'Beggars can't be choosers, Nell. If you're game to risk it, so am I.'

So when the party ended an hour or so later, with children scrambling for the last crumbs of cake and the barrel organist having to be restrained from playing 'God Save the King', Violet and I came to be sitting side by side in a horse cab, along with the Princess Sophia, on the way to the scarcely-known land on the north side of Hampstead Heath. There were so many trays and kettles piled up round us that we looked like a travelling ironmonger's. A large ladle was digging into my kneecap and Violet was holding a string bag of ham bones.

'Anna will use them for the soup,' said Sophia. 'You know we grow all our own food, except for the meat?' She thought about it for a while then added, 'And the bread and butter and some of the cheese.' She sighed. 'But then, we haven't been here so long.'

I noticed that as we left the scene of the street party behind us she was growing more subdued. The horse was ambling along, but she made no attempt to hurry up the driver.

'One day we shall grow and make everything we need – all our own food, our own clothes, then more food to give to people who are hungry. Nobody should be hungry on an earth that can grow so much food, nobody.'

She clasped her hands and stared at us, her round eyes sad.

'When I was a little girl at home I'd ride my pony through the fields and woods all day, sunrise to sunset . . .' One hand wafted free in a rocking motion, sketching fold upon fold of feudal contours. '. . . and all around me, all day, our people working for each other, loving each other.'

And then her father had spoilt it by freeing his serfs and she'd gone wandering through Europe ever since, trying to recreate something that had perhaps only existed in a child's imagination.

'Tell me about the cart,' I said.

She dragged herself back from her Russian fields and looked at me, more warily.

'It was just a little idea, because people were making so much fuss about crowning a king, as if that would make any difference to anything. We wanted to remind them that kings are nothing – that they can do away with their kings and their police chiefs and their governors of prisons and live as free people.'

There was a long cab journey ahead of us, very long at this pace, so I decided to let her tell the story at her own speed. So far she'd given no indication that there was anything on the cart more dangerous than papier mâché. Let her keep to that for a while.

'Why not wait until coronation day itself? Why choose our march?'

'Your march? Oh, I see. On coronation day there would be too many police about on the streets, too many soldiers. We shouldn't get near Whitehall. So when we heard about the suffragettes' march we decided to join in at the back.'

Sensible enough so far, and much as I'd guessed.

'What was the idea exactly?'

She smiled, as if it still gave her pleasure in spite of what had happened.

'Oh, a little pantomime for the people. They'd drive up Whitehall and stop at the place where you cut off the head of your King Charles. Then when all the people were crowded round, Veronica would make a speech telling them how they were better off without kings, and they'd cut off the king's head. It was big, you remember, like this?' Her arms sketched a wide circle round her own head. 'When

113

the executioner shouted, Robert would duck down inside the body, like this' – she hunched her shoulders – 'and off would come the head.'

'Then?'

She stared.

'Then they'd just trot away.'

Unless the crowd lynched them or the police arrested them first. Even taking it at its face value it would have been an unpopular demonstration in a crowd hungry for pageantry. I let that pass and concentrated on the new name.

'Who's Veronica?'

She sighed. 'Poor Veronica, she loved him so much.'

'Loved whom?'

She looked at me as if I should have known.

'Loved Robert. So tragic, poor girl, and she's being so brave. You must be kind when you meet her. We must all be kind, like a family.'

I nodded as solemnly as I could, but felt the same surge of excitement as when I'd seen the unicorn on the picture. If this was right, then Veronica was a witness and I was going to meet her.

'Which was she, the knight or the unicorn?'

'The unicorn. She'd have taken the head off when it was time to speak.'

'And Veronica got back safely, after what happened?'

I remembered the cart careering away across the bridge, the lion at the reins, the knight restraining the unicorn from jumping.

'They all got back safely, apart from the driver. He ran away, stupid man.'

'But they had to abandon the cart.'

'We thought that might happen. We had – arrangements, friends they could go to.'

She was cagey about that and not surprisingly. Of course they'd have made some sort of escape arrangements for after the explosion, supposing any of them survived it. I went on asking questions as if there'd been nothing more to it than her pantomime.

114

'So all five of the people on your cart came from your commune?'

'Yes, of course.'

Robert Withering, who was dead. A woman called Veronica, who had loved him. A knight in cardboard armour, a lion and an executioner.

'If it hadn't been for that lion they'd have all been arrested at the bridge.'

'Anna's a brave woman. She's Russian, like me.'

The same Anna who would boil up the ham bones for soup? A most resourceful lion. The princess gave another sigh.

'They were all brave people.'

'And yet one of them,' I said, 'shot Robert Withering.'

She'd had time to think about it since I first put the idea to her at the party, or time to get angry. Violet gave me a worried look. I watched Sophia's face change from pride to unhappiness.

'You said so. Why should any of us shoot Robert?'

'You know them all. I don't.'

She knew them all, and yet she hadn't dismissed what I'd said out of hand. Certainly she'd started by blaming the police, but that was only to be expected. Here was I, a stranger, accusing one of her associates of murder and she was listening to me. More than listening, giving me a look that implored me to say it wasn't true. I said, as gently as I could manage:

'You've been worried about it yourself, haven't you?'

An infinitesimal nod. There were tears in her eyes again.

'Is that because there's a reason why somebody might want to kill Robert Withering?'

'We all loved him, admired him.'

'All?'

Her silence was the answer.

'Was there one person in particular on the cart who might have wanted to kill him?'

She burst out, 'How can I tell you? He came to us when he was in trouble. We took him in.'

115

He, so neither the lion nor the unicorn.

'The knight or the executioner?'

'Executioner, no. Turnip's a good man, when he doesn't drink too much.'

'Who was the knight, then?'

She hesitated a long time before replying.

'Michael's an unhappy man, but I didn't think he would kill anybody.'

So the princess thought a man called Michael might have killed Withering. From the way she was talking, she'd suspected it days before I'd spoken to her, perhaps as soon as the actors in her pantomime made their way back.

'Have you asked any of them about it?'

'How can I? If you live with people, work with people, eat with people, how can you ask them – did you kill our friend, our brother? And supposing he says yes, what do you do? Do you call the police?'

Her fists were bunched, her voice had gone higher.

'And yet you want to know, don't you?'

She dropped her head, looking down at the kettles packed round her feet.

'You will find out for me. Don't tell anybody else, tell me.'

It was the invitation I needed, but there was something to be settled first. I waited until she was looking up at me again.

'Yes, I'll find out for you if I can. But I won't get far if you're not honest with me.'

'Honest? What is there to be but honest?'

'You haven't been, though. We've been talking as if that cart were only a kind of travelling theatre. It was more than that, wasn't it?'

'What do you mean?'

She was giving a good performance of puzzlement.

'The king, Robert Withering that is, was sitting on something.'

'Crates, boxes, something like that. But . . .'

'Crates or boxes packed with enough dynamite to blow up Scotland Yard. Shouldn't we admit that at the start?'

116

If I'd ever seen genuine surprise on a face I saw it then. Her jaw dropped and the natural colour drained out of her face, leaving only the poppy gash of rouge on her lips, two round patches of rouge stranded high on her cheeks. She began to pitch forward. Violet gasped and put an arm round her shoulder to save her.

'You shouldn't have done that, Nell. She's an old woman.'

She sat there holding the princess, making soothing noises, looking reproachfully at me. It was some time before Sophia spoke and when she did it came out as a series of gasps.

'I don't know anything about dynamite.'

The problem was that I more than half believed her.

THIRTEEN

VIOLET'S ARM STAYED ROUND HER, while I tried not to feel ashamed of myself and reconsidered.

'Did the police say that?'

Sophia was recovering a little and fighting back, though not strongly.

'The police, yes, but somebody else as well. Somebody I trust.'

That was what I'd been considering, and I'd come to the conclusion that I trusted both Geraldine and her sources of information. In her rarefied circle, where the politicians needn't take the trouble to lie to each other, it was common knowledge that Withering had died in the attempt to blow up Scotland Yard. Brust alone I'd have disbelieved on instinct, Inspector Merit more reluctantly. When Brust, Merit and Geraldine all said the same thing I'd take it as a fact until proved otherwise. Then there was the princess's reaction.

'It shocks you? You really didn't know?'

She shook her head.

'Would you have disapproved, though? After all, I take it that you are against police forces.'

'Of course I am. Police are only there to protect rich people against poor people.'

'Something in that,' Violet murmured. I could see she was still annoyed with me.

'So would you have approved of blowing up Scotland Yard?'

I warned myself that I must guard against doing to her

what Brust had done to Simon, translating political theory into murderous fact. She thought for some time before answering.

'Dynamite doesn't choose. If you must kill a person, then it's better to shoot him. There were people there, not just policemen?'

Not pausing to debate whether policemen were people, I assured her quite truthfully that there had been crowds of people watching the procession, including children.

'And there must have been a real risk that the whole thing would explode before they got to Scotland Yard. There was a fire on the cart just as they were coming over the bridge. The executioner stamped it out. Did they tell you that when they got back?'

She shook her head. Some of the colour was coming back to her face.

'And you honestly thought that it was just a tableau on that cart?'

'Yes, of course I did. Do you think I'd have let poor Veronica go on it if I thought there was dynamite?'

She was indignant, but I noticed she didn't include the useful Anna in her concern. What was special about Veronica, apart from her love for Withering?

'Tell me more about the tableau. Who planned it?'

'We all planned it. We do everything together, like a family.'

'Robert Withering was one of them?'

'Of course.'

'Who designed the costumes?'

'Glass.'

There was a hesitation before she said the word.

'Glass, is that a man or a woman?'

'A man.'

'Has he got another name?'

'Just Glass.'

It came out coldly and I sensed that there was no point in asking her more about him. It wouldn't be unusual for an anarchist to have a *nom de guerre*.

'How did you choose the people to be on the tableau?'

'Nobody chose. It's not like the army. People are not ordered to do things. They do whatever's necessary.'

'But it emerged somehow that there'd be five people – the king, the lion and unicorn, the knight and the executioner. You knew in advance who they were going to be?'

'Yes. Robert would be the king. Veronica would be the unicorn and do the talking because she has a good clear voice, then Anna and Turnip for the others.'

'And Michael?'

Michael, the unhappy man. Her candidate, although she hadn't said so, for shooting Withering if she had to accept that one of her family was to blame.

'Michael wanted to go, he insisted on going.'

'You didn't want him to?'

'It wasn't a case what I wanted or didn't.'

'Who then?'

'Some of the others didn't want him.'

I was sure there was more to it than that, but she wasn't going to tell me and I didn't want to be distracted from the main point.

'Where was the cart put together?'

'In our commune, in the old coach shed.'

'Who built it?'

'Everybody.'

'When did it leave your commune?'

'Saturday afternoon, early. Robert said we had to allow plenty of time because the horse was slow.'

'And the five of them were on the cart when it left?'

'Yes. Not in their places, like they'd be in Whitehall, just sitting on the cart.'

'In their costumes?'

'Yes.'

'The dynamite was under the dais where the king was sitting. Was the dais on the cart then?'

'Of course. It was all ready. We were proud of it because it looked so good.'

If all five of them had been in league they could have

120

stopped somewhere between Muswell Hill and Westminster and loaded up the dynamite, but it would have been far easier to do it before they left the commune. One of the five at least would have had to know about it so that he or she could light the fuse. Then what was supposed to happen? Would the figures in their costumes jump off and run away at the last minute before the explosion, or didn't it matter? There were fanatics who might consider lives well sacrificed in revenge for Sidney Street, but from the little I'd seen of the princess so far, I found it hard to associate her with that.

There was silence in the cab as it threaded its way northwards. Then Violet glanced out of the window and gasped and I realised that we were moving slowly with the traffic up Holloway Road and would be passing within a few hundred yards of the prison gates. My clothes felt clammy and I had to clench my hands together to stop them shaking. We couldn't ask the cab to turn round now without attracting attention to ourselves. Anyway, if you looked at it logically we were in no more danger there than anywhere, probably less since the police would expect us to be miles away by now. Three respectable women in a cab returning from charitable work among the children of the East End, two escaping prisoners and one anarchist. It was a sharp reminder that we needed the princess's charity to hide us, as well as her information. As we passed the turning to the prison Violet screwed her eyes up and pushed herself back against the seat, like an animal hiding from a beam of light. It was the princess's turn to comfort her.

'Poor Violet. We shall look after you.'

I thought that the police would be questioning all my friends in the suffragette movement. They'd be puzzled and grieved by what I'd done. If there ever would be a time when I could explain, it seemed from that point in the Holloway Road unimaginably far away.

Once we were past it and climbing up towards Highgate I tried to pull myself out of my depression and get on with the work.

'You realise that if you want me to find out what happened to Robert Withering I shall have to ask people questions?'

'Let them talk to you of their own accord. Don't ask them questions like a policewoman.'

'Shall you tell them what I'm trying to do?'

A violent shake of the head.

'No. We shall tell them the truth – that you have escaped from prison. They will welcome you.'

Not quite all, I thought.

'What about Glass?'

I was probing, after her reaction when we first talked about him. This time her alarm was obvious.

'He mustn't know. Glass has had some very bad times with police. He will be sure you're a police spy.'

'Why?'

'He thinks that about everybody. He's been betrayed very often, you see.'

'If he thinks I'm a police spy, what will he do?'

She turned her head away.

'You must be careful. We shan't tell Glass what we've been talking about. I shall say I met you in Stepney and you asked me to help, that's all. You understand?'

She put her hand on my knee. More than alarm in the grip – fear. Yes, I said, I understood. The cab rolled on past the leafy gardens and new brick villas of Muswell Hill. She leaned out to give directions to the driver and we turned into a rutted lane with a tall hawthorn hedge on the left and a high brick wall on the right. Another direction to the driver and we came to a halt outside a wide double door in the wall. It looked as if it had once been the carriage entrance to a substantial house, but the green paint was blistered and flaking. We got down into the lane with our jugs and kettles and ham bones and the cab rolled away in a cloud of dust. The princess gave a deep sigh, squared her shoulders under the flowered shawl, and knocked sharply on her own back door.

We had to wait for some time. There was a scraping sound

122

on the other side of the door and I noticed that a hatch had been drawn back from a peephole newly bored into the old wood. Nobody was taking us on trust, even if the princess was expected back. The man who eventually opened one of the gates to us didn't look like most people's idea of an anarchist. He was in his late thirties or early forties, clean shaven, with an active, straight-backed look about him. He wore dark trousers and a waistcoat neatly buttoned over a rough cotton shirt with the sleeves rolled up and secured with binder twine, brown boots that were worn but highly polished. He held a metal rod in his hand like a steward's wand of office, with a smell wafting off it.

'Is it the drains again, Digby?'

'Yes, drains it is.' I had the feeling that his instinct was to add 'ma'am' and he was learning to resist it. 'The women will keep letting the potato peelings get down the sink, in spite of me telling them.'

Some things, obviously, anarchism didn't change. When the drains get blocked, it's always the women's fault. Still, there was a comforting solidity about Digby. I could see that the princess felt it too as she let him take some of the pans she was carrying. He looked Violet and myself up and down, not unfriendly, but shrewd. The princess introduced us.

'That's Violet and this is Nell. They're coming to stay with us for a while.'

That seemed to be all the explanation needed.

We were standing in a big enclosed yard behind a three-storey, brick-built house. There was a coach house and several loose boxes along one side. No horses visible. Chickens pecked in the dust and a large gander hissed at us from a manure heap. The house itself was solid nineteenth-century with brickwork patterns round the windows and terracotta dragons on the roof. It looked dilapidated, with several window panes boarded up and pink valerian growing from rootholds on crumbling ledges. Apart from Digby, the yard was deserted.

'They're all inside having their dinner. I said I'd do a turn while I was seeing to the drains and have mine later.'

A turn of what, I wondered. Guard duty? With its high brick wall and solid gates this side of the house looked proof against anything short of a battering ram.

Sophia led the way up some steps and into the back of the house. Sounds of washing up were coming from a half-open doorway on our left. Violet pulled a face at me and murmured, 'Not again.' There were two women at the sink and a baby in a wicker-work crib on the kitchen table behind them, among piles of plates. One of them was very young with a round face, breasts straining against her bodice and masses of tumbling dark hair. The other was in her thirties, square and powerfully built, with high cheekbones, a strong jaw and eyes that challenged Violet and me to give an account of ourselves as soon as we walked into the room. Sophia saved us the trouble.

'Hello, Anna. Hello, Serafina. Nell and Violet have escaped from Holloway so they're coming to stay with us.'

The younger woman, Serafina, gave us a sweet, uncomprehending smile. Anna dried her hands on her dark skirt and looked at Sophia sourly.

'Where will they sleep? There's no space in our room.'

The voice was as deep as a man's with an accent I didn't recognise, probably Russian. I looked at the set of her shoulders and her big, capable hands.

'I've seen you before,' I said, 'only you won't have seen me. You had other things to think about at the time.'

Her expression didn't change.

'I saw you. You were running along in the road. You had a blue dress on.'

The way she said it was neither friendly nor hostile, just factual. She was right too, which proved two things: that she had a remarkably cool head in a crisis and saw no need to hide the fact that she'd been on the cart. Sophia broke in hastily, as if she hadn't expected me to start work straight away.

'They'll be hungry. We must find them some dinner.'

'There's no pie left.'

124

'Then we must find them something else. Where's Veronica?'

'Upstairs, I suppose.'

There'd been tenderness in Sophia's question, but there was none in Anna's reply.

'How is she?'

'Well enough to help us in the kitchen – if she wanted to.'

'We must be kind to her, poor girl. She'll do her share of the work when she can.'

Anna gave her a curl of the lip and went over to a big meat safe in the corner, taking her time. In spite of her square build she trod lightly, swaying her hips as she walked. The princess watched, embarrassed by this reluctant hospitality. I sensed there might be an atavistic itch for the time when there were serfs to obey orders, but she kept her own rules. I sensed something else too. She might have asked me to find out for her who killed Robert Withering, but I couldn't expect any support from her now that we were in the commune. She was shrewdly distancing herself, leaving it to Anna to introduce us to the others. Sophia wasn't in charge, which in an anarchist commune was only right and proper – in theory. Free people united in a common interest don't need leaders and don't need laws. All very well, but Withering had been shot and the princess was scared.

'I think I'll go and look for Veronica.'

Anna, her back to us, only shrugged. Sophia stayed just long enough to stroke the baby's cheek then left us to it.

After an interval of plate crashing, Anna cleared a space for us on the kitchen table. There was a kind of yeasty smell about her, like a bakery when the dough's rising, not unpleasant. She produced some slices of gritty bread, goat's cheese, limp spring onions and a bottle of plum brandy.

'We make nearly all our food ourselves.'

The princess had been proud of that but Anna sounded gloomy and when I tasted the cheese I could see why. The plum brandy was the best of the meal, but I had to go carefully with that. Anna, on the other hand, drank half a tumbler-full with no obvious effect. Serafina went on with her work at the sink, stopping now and then to tickle the baby.

'So what are you doing here?' Anna said.

I gave her a much-edited version of my arrest and our escape. She nodded from time to time, but I had an idea that she didn't believe me. She made no comment at all when I told her about Simon's arrest for shooting Withering. I could see Violet glancing at me, clearly wanting me to go carefully, but there wasn't time for caution.

'You must have known Robert Withering well,' I said.

She shrugged.

'Who do you think shot him?'

Another shrug.

'The police.'

From the way she said it I knew it was a routine reply, an article of faith. If she had any real ideas on the subject she certainly didn't intend to share them with me. Not so far, at least.

It was probably still early evening, but I'd lost sense of time. Either the food or the brandy or the chance to sit down at last brought warm currents of sleep drifting over me, so that it was as much as I could do to keep my chin off the table. Violet keeled over against me, quietly and without fuss, and went to sleep on my shoulder.

'I'll find beds for you.'

Was there just a touch of sympathy in Anna's deep voice? We roused ourselves and followed her into a corridor that looked as if it ran the length of the house. The door in the middle that would once have closed off the polite apartments from the servants' quarters was propped open, its baize covering hanging in tatters. The only light in the corridor came from a window over the door at the far end, glass panels in mauve, yellow and green showing a galleon on stormy seas. There was a solid, dark wood staircase ahead of us and various doors off the corridor. The floor was cluttered with all kinds of things, a broken hoe, a hatchet and a pile of kindling, a black bundle that looked like an old rug but, when I stubbed my toe against it in the half-dark, turned out to be a sleeping dog. It gave me a reproachful look and went to sleep again.

There were three or four men in the downstairs corridor, doing nothing much but smoking cigarettes and talking quietly. They looked at us with curiosity and stood aside to let us pass. They were all much alike, young and dark and bearded, with a hollow look round the eyes that suggested food and sleep were in short supply. I glanced in at an open door and saw austere metal-framed bunks, as in a barracks, with grey blankets spread casually around. They'd never pass inspection in Holloway.

Anna stopped about half-way along the corridor and opened a narrow door on a flight of stone steps descending. We followed her to a semi-basement floor where the rooms were almost cellars, with only narrow windows along the very top of the walls. She found her way without trouble in the dim light to a small room that smelt of damp earth and old distemper, produced matches from her pocket and lit a couple of stubby candles, revealing piles of broken furniture including several iron bedsteads.

'Here you are.'

She helped us to put the two least broken ones together, propping them up with random pieces from the other detritus. In an alcove outside a door she found a couple of dampish, straw-filled sacks for mattresses and two worn grey blankets. By the time we'd assembled all this she was less sullen and even produced something like a joke.

'Good beds, eh? Better than prison?'

Then she left us. We heard her feet tapping quickly up the stairs and the door closing. We slept.

I woke to darkness and soft footsteps outside. At first I thought I was back in prison with a wardress on her soft-soled rounds, then I knew I couldn't be because the darkness was so complete, not a shape or a hint of light to tell the eyes where to focus. Violet's whisper came at me out of the darkness.

'Nell, there's somebody outside.'

She sounded scared and so was I. No point in looking for the candle stubs because they'd have burned out long since and even to move in the dark would bring avalanches of broken furniture crashing down.

'Don't worry, it's probably Anna or the princess to make sure we're all right.'

Then the door opened suddenly and light rushed in like an attack. It was only a paraffin lamp, but after the total darkness it was dazzling, stupefying. I couldn't see the lamp at first, or the person behind it, but I knew this suddenness meant hostility. I must have put my hands to my eyes, because I saw through my fingers a shape coming into the room, putting the lamp down on a packing case then standing behind it.

'So you say you've escaped from Holloway?'

It was a man's voice, harsh with a sneer to it. An accent from somewhere in the English midlands.

'Yes.'

I tried to sound calm, almost managed it.

'Difficult, was it?'

'We were lucky.'

'Very lucky.'

He moved a little aside from the lamp, so that I could see him at last. A man in his thirties, shorter than average, with broad shoulders but none of the robustness that usually goes with them. A stooping way of standing made him seem even shorter than he was and he pushed his head towards us as short-sighted people do, although he wore wire-rimmed glasses. Like most of the rest of the men he was bearded, although in his case it was more like the fringe on a mantelpiece, looking as if it were in danger of losing its grip on his pink and shiny face.

'So how did you know to come here?'

I'd placed the accent now. Black Country, from around Wolverhampton way.

'A friend took me to Princess Sophia.'

He was shifting from one foot to another, looking at us. He reminded me of a portrait of Henry the Eighth, but a gnomelike version.

'What friend?'

'No business of yours.'

I threw back the blanket and swung my stockinged feet out of bed, so that I could sit up and look at him. Violet and I had both been too tired to undress. I noticed that she was still lying there under the blanket, trying to make sense of him.

'Everything's my business.'

'The princess invited us here . . .'

'We don't have princesses.'

'Very well, Sophia invited us here and promised us her protection. I'm sure she'll be delighted to discuss it with you in the morning. Meanwhile we're very short of sleep and we'd appreciate it if you'd leave us in peace.'

He stared at me for a while, then a slow smile stretched his face.

'In peace. I like that. You be careful. You be very careful.'

He was trying to stare me out. Silly game. I smiled then deliberately turned my head away.

'What are you grinning at?'

'Was I? I'm sorry.'

He picked up the lamp and backed towards the door, still staring at me. I hadn't seen him blink, not once. Perhaps his skin was too tight to let the eyes close.

'I suppose you know our names.'

'I know the names you're going under.'

'So perhaps we could ask yours.'

He paused at the doorway, lamp in hand.

'Glass,' he said.

He closed the door as he went, leaving darkness more stifling than before.

'Strewth,' said Violet, 'I don't suppose he gets many invitations to play Father Christmas.'

And we slept again.

FOURTEEN

IT WAS PROBABLY AROUND SIX in the morning when the clamour started. It sounded like somebody banging on a saucepan with a ladle, first above our heads inside the house then outside in the yard. I sat up ready to do battle, thinking it was another nocturnal visit from the man called Glass, but saw that light was filtering through the cobwebs over our slit of window. Violet lifted a startled head from the blanket. Her hair had turned into a frizzy halo and there were dark rings round her eyes. I suppose I looked worse. We put on our awful shoes and staggered up the cellar steps and into the hallway. People were coming from all the downstairs rooms, yawning and stretching. A normal reveille at least, not an emergency.

We went past them into the air of the back yard and found more people in the same state coming from the outhouses. I counted eighteen altogether, fourteen men and four women, including Anna and the young Italian woman, Serafina, with her baby in her arms. There was a pump and trough in the corner of the yard where a small queue had formed of people drinking from cupped hands, sluicing water into their faces. A bearded man in a flat cap was pumping and the water came in spurts, so it was a matter of chance whether you got a trickle or a flood into your hands. Violet and I joined the queue, getting a few curious glances but no more than that.

With the high brick wall closing off the yard you couldn't see much more of the world outside than from the exercise area in Holloway. I felt as if I hadn't washed for weeks and

130

envied the young man at the front of the queue who, unlike the rest, stripped his shirt off and dashed double handfuls of water over chest, face and hair then shook like a spaniel so that water drops shone in the sun round him. His face and neck were as brown as breadcrust, his chest white. His feet were bare too and he turned up his trouser legs, jumped into the trough and paddled. There was an air of life and enjoyment about him that made him stand out from the rest. Some of the men in the queue told him to hurry up and get out, so that they could have their turn. They called him Jimmy. He answered good humouredly in a Liverpool accent and splashed like a sparrow in a puddle.

I noticed that he'd left his discarded shirt and boots on the ground, near where Violet and I were standing. I suppose my own annoying shoes and the blisters on my feet from the day before made me more than usually conscious of footwear. In any other circumstances they wouldn't have attracted a second look, being no more than workmen's brown leather boots, unpolished for a long time and very scuffed. But they weren't just scuffed, they were burned. There was a black scorch across the toe of one of them. The other had been left flung on its side, with the sole showing, and that was scorched too. I remembered the cart, the fire, the executioner stamping it out.

'What's up, Nell?'

Violet. Either she'd read my thoughts or I'd made some sound.

'That man.'

'Yes. First good thing I've seen for weeks.'

Jimmy had got out of the trough by now and was doing a sort of hornpipe to get his feet dry. When he'd finished he came walking over to where he'd left his shirt and boots which meant towards us. His grin turned itself on us, lingered on me then adjusted itself downwards six inches to Violet.

'Morning. Where did you drop from?'

'Out of the sky.' Violet smiled back at him. 'What about you?'

'Another bit of the sky, called Bootle. Jimmy's my name, Jimmy Kelly.'

'You always so cheerful?'

'That's right. Hard work and a clear conscience, that's me.'

Looking at him you would have thought his conscience was as clear as the water drops he'd been shaking off his body.

'When do we get breakfast, then?'

'After we've done a bit of work. But you can have these to be going on with.'

He moved close to her, feeling in his pocket, then his hand brushed hers. He winked, moved away and started putting on his shirt, leaving her staring at something in her hand.

'Strawberries. Now how on earth did he get those?'

Three of them, small but ripe. When she saw a man behind us in the queue was taking some interest, she slid them quickly into her pocket.

'We'll share those later.'

In a few minutes it was our turn at the pump.

'Don't they have toothbrushes in this place?'

'I don't know. Violet, be careful. Leave him to me.'

'I saw him first.'

That fairly took my breath away. I was going to explain about the executioner and the boots, but Anna was standing near us so I gave up.

We washed as best we could and I decided not to try to put up my hair. Anna and the few other women present wore theirs loose over their shoulders and anyway I'd lost most of my pins. By then most of the others had disappeared through a narrow alleyway between two outhouses. Violet and I followed them and found ourselves in a large kitchen garden of about two acres, surrounded by the same high brick wall that closed in the yard. A lot of care and money must have been spent on the garden about half a century ago, but now only a few reminders of them were left. A line of glass–houses with missing panes sagged along the south-facing wall. Espaliered pears and peaches had broken away from their moorings and staggered over paths that were more weed than gravel. In the centre a stone nymph clutching draperies to her chest, ineffectively, was marooned in the bowl of a dry fountain. Snow-white goats browsed on sow thistle and cow parsley among ancient currant bushes. I noticed the remains of a strawberry bed, which at least explained Jimmy's gift to Violet.

In spite of it all, there had been some recent attempts at cultivation. Potatoes and onions looked flourishing and marrow plants were making a successful fight against convolvulus. There was a large patch of lettuces too, partly weeded, and that was where the day's work had started. A dozen or so people were already hoeing between the rows, working doggedly but without particular enthusiasm. I recognised Digby, the solid man who'd let us in the night before, an empty pipe clenched between his teeth. And, working on his own with as much distance as possible between him and the others, a young man with a bulging forehead and wispy beard. I stared at him until I noticed that Digby was watching me. There were hoes leaning against a post, almost new ones. I picked up one and handed another to Violet.

'What's this for?'

'The dignity of manual labour.'

'Dignity? What's hoeing got to do with dignity? Anyway, I thought anarchists went round throwing bombs, not weeding bloody lettuces.'

I decided not to waste energy educating Violet in anarchist theory, because I was puzzled myself. I thought about it as we hoed. I knew several people who described themselves as anarchists and they were, on the whole, gentle souls who believed that once governments melted away, the essential goodness and sociability of humankind would take over. Princess Sophia had struck me as definitely one of those. Lettuce-eating anarchists, you might say, rather than the carnivorous kind. Some of our fellow lettuce weeders must be of the carnivorous variety, but the cultivation, the goats, the baby, the fact that they'd let us in at all, went oddly with dynamite.

While I was puzzling this, and making no progress except in weed reduction, Violet must have drifted away from me. When I next looked up I saw that she'd taken herself over where Jimmy was working. He was showing her how to use a hoe and the lesson apparently required him to stand behind her and keep his hands on her hips. Some of the people round them were smiling, but I noticed Anna watching sourly. Then she looked towards the brick archway and her expression became even sourer. I followed her eyes and saw a young, dark-haired woman with a pale, tragic face and red rings round her eyes. She paused to pick up a hoe then came walking along the lettuce rows, looking at nobody, noticing nothing. But you could tell, even at a distance, that she had washed in a more thorough and leisurely way than the rest of us. You could practically smell the soap on her. Her hair, although pulled severely back from her face and twisted up into a knot, was as clean and glossy as a horse chestnut fresh out of its case. She wore a russet coloured skirt and rough white blouse very similar to those of the other women, but hers looked freshly laundered. Even after she'd started hoeing she still stood out from the rest of us. I envied her cleanness and didn't blame Anna if she felt the same. Then I saw she'd turned her attention to the man on his own with the bulging forehead. He was watching the woman who'd just arrived with hunger in every line of his body, although she hadn't even looked at him. I moved closer to Anna.

'Who is she?'

'Veronica.'

She said it in a mincing kind of way, all the syllables equal and like pinches.

'The one who loved Robert Withering?'

Anna gave me a look full of dislike, for me, Veronica or both and turned away. The man who'd been watching Veronica was attacking docks with his sickle in a frenzy of blows, as if the only thing that mattered in the world were their destruction.

I needed some names and I looked round my fellow workers wondering who might help. Anna, it was obvious, didn't want to talk. Jimmy would be talkative, but I wanted to find out more about him first. In the absence of the princess herself that left only one acquaintance. Decapitating groundsel as I went, I worked my way over until I was hoeing alongside Digby.

'Hello, lass. Doing all right?'

There were traces of a Yorkshire accent in his voice, but from some time back. He took his empty pipe out of his mouth and put it in his back pocket.

Yes thank you, I said. We talked for a while about things that didn't matter, the weather, the weeds. He seemed as calm and unworried as a man working his allotment. I wondered how he came to be there. It had struck me already that some of the princess's commune were there because they needed a refuge rather than from political conviction. If so, questions would be unwelcome, but I had to try.

'What's the name of that man over there?'

He glanced.

'Michael.'

I'd been right, then. The same man who'd been the knight on the dynamite cart. The man the princess thought – although she wouldn't say it – might possibly have shot Robert Withering.

'He looks unhappy.'

'He might have a good reason.'

'Not like Jimmy Kelly.'

Violet's lesson in horticulture seemed to be making progress. Jimmy was teasing her, some of the others watching and laughing.

'He's always happy.'

'Is he the one they call Turnip?'

The princess had said there were four people on the cart: Veronica, Michael, Anna and Turnip. I knew from the way Digby was staring at me that I'd taken a wrong turn.

'Turnip? What makes you think that?'

'I thought I heard one of the other men call him that.'

He bent down to disentangle a stalk of fumitory from a lettuce.

'No. Not him.'

'Which one's Turnip then?'

He straightened up and looked round.

'Can't see him. He's probably sleeping it off as usual. Why did you want him?'

'I don't, particularly, I was just curious about the name.'

He felt in his pocket for his pipe. This time, instead of sucking on it emptily, he took a thin yellow oilskin pouch from his back pocket, carefully peeled off one wafer of pressed tobacco and divided it precisely in half with his thumbnail. Half went carefully back into the pouch.

'Let me give you a word of advice. Don't be too curious about names here. If somebody chooses to call himself something that's his own affair, and he's probably got a reason for it, even if it isn't what you'd call a good reason.'

He looked at me as he rolled the tobacco to shreds between his palms.

'I see. Like Glass?'

His face changed. He'd seemed quite relaxed until then.

'You be careful with him. You don't want to attract that one's attention.'

'Why?'

'He doesn't like people asking questions about him.'

'Because of things he's done?'

'That's just the kind of question not to ask.'

'Is he in charge here?'

'Nobody's in charge – so they say.'

136

'But people are scared of him?'

He nodded, then looked away. We worked side by side in silence for a while, until a shout went up from the other side of the patch: 'Breakfast time.'

People put down their hoes and went, all but one. Michael stayed where he was, still slashing at weeds with his sickle, but so ineffectively by now that most of the stems were cut only half through and drooped back on themselves, swinging from fleshy hinges. I waited until Digby and the others had disappeared through the archway and went over to him. He didn't look up until I spoke to him.

'My name's Nell. I saw you eight days ago on Westminster Bridge. I don't suppose you saw me.'

'Westminster Bridge?'

'You were trying to blow up Scotland Yard, remember? Or do you do that every day?'

His eyes hardly focused on me, wild eyes. He might in other circumstances have been a tolerably handsome man, but now he was so strung up and desperate that it hurt to look at him.

'You're . . . you're the one who escaped from Holloway?'

'You were trying to stop Veronica jumping off the cart, after Withering had been shot.' No time for subtlety. 'I suppose she wanted to go to Withering. You were right, of course. She couldn't have done anything. He was dead by then.'

He screwed up his eyes, as if that would give him time to think.

'You wanted to protect her and she wanted to protect Robert Withering. And you were both of you sitting on a cart load of dynamite.'

'Oh God.' He opened his eyes and seemed to focus on me for the first time.

'Take her away from here. Get her away from here.'

He dropped the sickle, took a few unsteady steps and sat down on a heap of couch grass piled up for burning. I went and sat beside him.

'Take Veronica away? Would she come, even if I could?'
'She's got to go away. Something's going to happen.'
'What?'
'To me. Or else the police will come first. It's only a matter of time, then it will be like Sidney Street, the police, the troops. He'll burn the place with us in it rather than surrender, like they did. He's said so.'
'Glass?'

He nodded. I thought he was right that it was only a matter of time before the police closed in. I imagined Brust questing northwards up Hampstead Heath, labrador nose twitching. If I'd been able to follow up the clue of the sheet, surely Scotland Yard would have done it by now. I asked him his name.

Michael, he said. Michael Peterson. He added the surname as if it came from another lifetime. His hand, large and square, blotched with the green juice of weeds, tugged at the couch grass.

'If you think that,' I said, 'why don't you take Veronica away while there's still time?'

'Because she wouldn't go with me. She might go with you, with anyone else.'

He seemed beyond humility even, as if he'd ceased to exist.

'But you feel responsible for her?'

He looked at me as if he were trying to make sense of the question.

'You see, it's my fault she's here.'

'Why is it your fault?'

He gave a long sigh then started mumbling to the dying weeds so that I had to bend my head close to him to hear.

'You'd need to know her parents, Veronica's parents. Her father's a fat ignoramus who thinks he's conquered the world because he owns a couple of clothes factories, mother a little religious mouse, always ill with something. Veronica wanted to go to college, do something with her life, but her father wouldn't think of it. He tried to buy her off with more music lessons – she's talented – which was where I came in.'

138

'You're a music teacher.'

'A lecturer at a teacher's college, not far from where they live. She'd outpaced her ordinary teacher, so father thought she needed something better. He got me for his money.'

'And . . .'

'Can't you guess? We fell in love. Over the piano score of *The Barber of Seville.*'

'Father didn't approve?'

'Of course not. He'd already got somebody mapped out for her – heir to a cheese importer, no less. He started spying at keyholes, caught us kissing and threw me out, literally. He's a big man. So of course after that there was nothing for it but to elope.'

'Veronica agreed?'

'It was her idea.'

I could understand that. He struck me as a man doomed to be defeated, the one who always gets the dud penny in his change, the umbrella with the hole.

'And you eloped to this place?'

'No, of course not. Not at first anyway. But you see, Veronica always had social ideals, not like her father. She hated being caged up by money and privilege. It wasn't just eloping because we loved each other, it was showing we could live a useful life, without depending on his money. A flight to freedom.'

'How were you going to live?'

'She'll be twenty-one in August. We can get married then, whatever her father says. I . . . at first I wanted to find lodgings for her, support her until then, but she . . . she said these were exactly the outworn conventions that we were running away from. She insisted that . . .'

'That you live together?'

He nodded.

'Then my college found out, so of course I was dismissed. So Veronica and I came to London together. We had enough money for a few weeks. We rented this awful room near Paddington station. The idea was that I should get work as a music teacher, but I had no references you see, not after being dismissed from the college. Veronica wanted to work as a typist, but you have to pay quite a lot of money to be trained. She didn't know that. She thought you could just sit down at a typewriter and do it. There were days when we didn't eat at all and there wasn't even a fireplace in that wretched room, even if we could have afforded coal. This was March and it was so cold.'

'You couldn't find work at all?'

'I got something after a while, in a theatre orchestra. I'd brought my violin with me. But the violin got broken when some drunk took it off me and tried to play it when I was walking home one night.'

'How did you come to this place?'

'Veronica started going to meetings. She'd cared about poverty before, we both had, but when you're living like we were you know it's the worst thing in the world, the cruellest thing. So when I was at the theatre she'd walk miles and miles to go to these meetings. Anyway, at one of them somebody told her about this community of people up in Muswell Hill who had no personal property and didn't believe in marriage and so on and worked with their hands for what they needed. She said we should go there.'

'You agreed?'

He spread out his fingers and looked at them. They were grimed and calloused.

'How could I disagree? I'd failed. I couldn't keep us. We just put the few things we had left in a paper bag and walked up here. It was either that or tell her to go back to her father, and she said she'd rather die than do that.'

I thought I saw a flicker of movement under the brick arch towards the house. When I turned to look, I couldn't see anybody.

'I think somebody might be watching us.'

'There usually is.'

He was too numbed to worry about it.

140

'When did you realise that it wasn't simply a socialist commune?'

'When that man arrived. Glass.'

'Wasn't Glass here when you came?'

'No, it was the princess and some others. It was an odd place and we could see the princess wasn't running it very well, but it seemed on the right lines and after that room in Paddington anywhere was an improvement. The princess took to Veronica at once, almost adopted her.'

'What about Robert Withering? Was he here then?'

He twisted at a handful of couch grass. His fingers were bleeding, cut by the sharp blades of it, but he didn't seem to notice.

'No, Withering wasn't here. He came later. He and Glass arrived together.'

'Were they friends?'

'Associates. The princess had met Withering in Geneva, more than a year back before she had to get out of there. She was besotted with the man. She kept talking about him to Veronica even before he got here, how intelligent he was, how brave he was, what a great revolutionary and so on. The man had practically bewitched her, but as you might have noticed, she's a very silly woman.'

'And a rich one?'

'She must have been once. I don't suppose there's much left by now except a few brooches and rings, and he'll get those even if he has to hack her fingers off to do it. I'm quoting his own words.'

'Glass again?'

'Yes. When Withering finally arrived from whatever he'd been doing abroad, he had Glass in tow. He made it clear to the princess that Glass was to get the same treatment that he got himself – orders obeyed and no questions asked.'

'How did the princess take that?'

'She had no choice.'

'And Veronica?'

He looked down at his hands and seemed to notice the

blood on them at last, but went on twisting at the sharp couch grass.

'Veronica fell hook, line and sinker in love with Robert Withering.'

That confirmed, at least, what I'd been told by Sophia.

'I could see what they were doing to her, what she was letting them do. I argued with her, but it didn't do any good, they just told her to stop having anything to do with me. They were drawing her into a little circle of their own, and it was my fault because I'd let her down. But you can't just stop loving somebody, even if she stops loving you.'

'You were jealous of Withering?'

'Jealous? It's a word. There's no word for what I felt about him. It's . . . I can't make anyone understand. You dream about it at night, you wake up in the morning and it's there. It twists your stomach, eats away at the spine . . . Call it jealous, if you like.'

'I suppose Withering and Veronica became lovers.'

He nodded. 'He didn't love her, though. That man couldn't love anyone. I think he and Glass worked it out together, as a way of tying her to them. He even lectured her about how love was meaningless and a man and a woman should just take each other's bodies when they needed, like taking money from a bank or food when you're hungry. No more than that.'

'Veronica accepted all that?'

'She thought she did. One night, you know what he did? He went to bed with Anna and let Veronica know he was doing it. Part of her education, he said. That night, I found her outside in the yard, crying. She pretended it was nothing to do with that, wouldn't speak to me. Then, much later, I saw Glass and Withering laughing together. I . . . I tried to hit him.'

'What happened?'

'They set on me, both of them. By the end of it I . . . I was begging for mercy. Can you understand what I felt about Withering?'

I said, 'In your place, I'd have wanted to kill him.'

FIFTEEN

HIS HEAD DROPPED.

'I don't think I'm the sort of man who kills people.'

It came out as an apologetic mumble to the ground.

'After all, you were trying to blow up Scotland Yard.'

He shook his head.

'Didn't you know there was dynamite on the cart?'

Another shake of the head. If he hadn't known, he didn't seem to care very much.

'What did you think you were trying to do?'

He sighed and started talking, still to the ground. It was much the same account I'd already heard from the princess, a drive into Whitehall on the tail of our procession, a ceremonial decapitation of the papier mâché king, a speech to any crowd that had gathered and a quick getaway.

'Did you want to be part of that, or were you ordered?'

'I knew Veronica would be in it so I had to go too.'

'How were the people chosen?'

'I don't know. When I found out what was supposed to be happening I went to Sophia and begged her to let me join it. I said I wanted to be there to protect Veronica.'

'Did you know Withering would be there too?'

'Yes.'

'And the princess let you go. Does that mean she was the one who planned it?'

'No, she doesn't plan anything. It was Glass and Withering. But sometimes they did what she asked in little things to keep her quiet.'

'Was anything said to you at all about Scotland Yard and dynamite?'

'No.'

'Do you think the princess knew?'

'I'm sure she didn't. She wouldn't have let Veronica go if she had.'

'Didn't it occur to you that it was a pretty silly thing you were doing in any case, this mock execution? Even if the crowd hadn't lynched you, you'd have all been arrested.'

'Yes, I was counting on that.'

'Counting on it?'

'It was the only chance I could see of getting Veronica away from here. If the police arrested us I could explain that it was all my fault and she . . .' He looked up at me for the first time.

'Well?'

'They'd have had to send her back to her parents.'

'I don't suppose she'd have thanked you for that.'

'It wouldn't have mattered, if I could only have got her away.'

I glanced towards the brick arch. If there was anybody watching us, he or she was invisible.

'So Sophia must have persuaded Glass and Withering to let you take part. What happened then?'

'Glass came to me on Saturday morning with the costume. There was some business about what I was supposed to do when we got to Whitehall. I didn't take much notice. I didn't care what they did.'

'What was his manner like? Did he seem excited?'

He stared at me.

'Does a snake get excited? He was just as he always is. I can remember the awful gloating look in his eyes when he threatened to have me killed, that's all.'

'Glass threatened to have you killed?'

'That's nothing new. He's obsessed with informers and police agents. He seemed to think I might be one, or pretended to. He said if anything went wrong, he'd know who to blame. Then he gave me a gun.'

He said it so flatly that it was some time before it
sank in.

'Glass gave you a gun? When?'

'On the Saturday afternoon, just before we got on the
cart. He said if the police tried to arrest us we shouldn't
be taken alive. He told me that some of the others would
have guns as well, and if I did anything to betray them,
they wouldn't hesitate to shoot me.'

'Was it loaded?'

'I suppose so. I don't know. I'd never had my hand on
a gun before.'

'What did you do with it?'

'He told me to tie it to my belt with a piece of string
and keep it tucked inside the waistband of my trousers,
under the armour.'

'What happened then?'

'All the others were on the cart. I got on it and
we went.'

'The others were in costume too?'

'Yes. I knew Veronica was going to be the unicorn and
Withering the king. I'd have recognised her anyway, her
hands, the way she stands, everything.'

'And the other two?'

'Anna didn't put the lion's head on until we got nearer
London because it was so hot. I knew she'd be there
anyway. She's Glass's spy.'

'How do you know that?'

'Veronica says so. She hates her.'

'So that was four of you. What about the executioner?'

'What about him?'

'Do you know who he was?'

'I think it was Turnip, but he kept his hood on all the
time and didn't say anything. He doesn't speak much
English at the best of times, even when he's sober.'

'So you're not sure it was Turnip?'

I thought of Jimmy Kelly and the singed boots.

'Does it matter?'

Did anything matter to him, except one thing?

'It's a long journey from here to Westminster. What happened?'

'Nothing. We just sat there.'

'You say you knew Veronica was the unicorn. Did you try to speak to her?'

'Several times. She wouldn't reply.'

'It would have been difficult, I suppose, through the unicorn's head.'

'She took that off for most of the journey. So did Withering. They were sitting there on the dais, with the heads beside them.'

On a stack of dynamite.

'Did they say anything to each other?'

He twisted at the grass until his hands were red. When he did answer, it sounded as if the words were being torn up by the roots.

'They whispered . . . sometimes. I could see they . . . were holding hands.'

'How did Veronica look?'

'She was . . . she was scared. He was trying to encourage her . . . he . . .'

It was so painful for him that I wanted to tell him to stop, that it didn't matter. But it did. Then a torrent of words came out.

'To sit there, a few feet away from her, wanting to protect her and have to watch him dragging her into it, deeper and deeper, seeing she was scared – can you imagine what that felt like?'

'But you did nothing?'

'What could I do. I . . . as we got to the places where there were more people I thought of jumping off and dragging her with me, only she wouldn't have come and . . .'

'And you thought at least some of the others had guns too?'

'Yes.'

'And it went on like this all the way to Westminster?'

'Yes. We went across the river and Withering showed us

146

the house we were supposed to make for if we were getting away from the police. Then they put the heads on and we crossed the river back again and . . . and it happened. You were there. You saw as much as I did.'

'I doubt it. I didn't see who shot Robert Withering.'

He looked at me, eyes still full of the pain of talking about Withering and Veronica.

'Neither did I.'

'But you were on the cart with them.'

'Yes, but I didn't see what happened.'

'Something caught fire as you were coming over Westminster Bridge. Did you see that?'

'Yes. I smelt burning and the sheets were smouldering and there was the executioner – Turnip or whoever it was – and Withering trying to stamp them out. Withering's head, the head he was wearing, was swaying about.'

'What did you do?'

'I tried to get hold of Veronica. I thought it was my chance to jump with her, while they were distracted. I got hold of her arm and . . . then it happened.'

'What?'

'I heard the shot and when I looked round Withering was swaying, falling over. Then another man I hadn't seen before got up on the cart and Withering fell onto him and . . . I think they both fell off together. Then . . . I think we must have turned round somehow.'

'That was Anna.'

'Yes. I had my hands full with Veronica. She wanted to jump off then, to go to him.'

'Did you know Withering was dead?'

'I thought so. We didn't know for sure until the next day. Glass got news of it somehow. Anyway, I managed to keep her on the cart and Anna drove it to the other side of the bridge and we left it there and ran to the house Withering had shown us. It was chaos. The people there were even more scared than we were, but they gave us ordinary clothes and got us away in the end.'

'What became of the gun Glass gave you?'

'I left it there. The people in the house told me to.'

'How did you get back here?'

'Veronica and I went together, by tram.'

'Did you have any money?'

A few days ago, that wouldn't have occurred to me. Some colour came into his face.

'I stole three shillings from a fruit monger's stall.'

'And the other two?'

'They must have come back some other way. Anna was here when we got here.'

'What about the executioner? Did you ever see him without his hood?'

He thought about it.

'No.'

'Didn't you think of trying to get Veronica away then, instead of coming back here?'

'Of course I tried. Coming back here was the last thing I wanted, but she wouldn't go anywhere else. She said she had to know what had happened to Withering. Now she knows he's dead she's got no reason to stay here any more. Can't you try to get her to go away with you?'

He was back there again, the only thing that mattered to him. There was one point that stuck out from his account and I came back to it.

'You say that when you actually heard the shot that killed Withering you had hold of Veronica's arm?'

'Yes.'

The reply came very promptly. Perhaps too promptly.

'In that case, it should follow that one of the other two shot Withering.'

'Yes. I suppose it should. What does it matter?'

'You're an intelligent man. You surely . . .'

'Have you ever been in love?'

'Yes.'

His look said, 'Then don't judge.' I thought that if he had fired the shot that killed Withering he was very close to admitting it. He was ready to say anything if I'd promise to help with Veronica.

148

'I asked you if you shot Withering and you said you don't think you're the kind of man who kills people. Aren't there times when anyone might kill?'

He looked at me with an odd twist of the lip, not quite a smile.

'If thoughts could kill, he'd have been dead the first time I saw them together.'

'Only thoughts?'

He said nothing. The first of the lettuce weeders were coming back through the arch from breakfast.

'If I told you I'd shot him, would you try to get Veronica to go away with you?'

'But is it true?'

He shrugged, stood up clumsily and looked round for his sickle.

'Ask her. Talk to her.'

Anna came along the path, swinging her hips and the hoe in rhythm, making no effort to hide her curiosity. As she passed us she gave both of us a slow smile. Michael turned away, looking physically sick.

'Is it something interesting he's telling you?'

When I didn't answer she walked on, still smiling to herself.

SIXTEEN

WE WORKED ALL THROUGH THE morning, with the flies circling and the sun climbing higher in a hazy sky. Veronica hadn't reappeared after breakfast and I made no more attempts to question anybody. It wasn't that I was so concerned about Anna, since what I was doing could hardly be kept secret, but because I had enough to think about. Michael would be mine for the asking, if only I'd promise to get Veronica away. In his present mood he'd walk tamely into Brust's lair or anywhere else, and even if he didn't confess to killing Withering his account would at least muddy the water enough to set Simon free. One certainly innocent man at liberty, in exchange for one probably innocent to put in a police cell. Not a bargain I could make. I didn't believe Michael had shot Withering. By his own account he had both gun and motive and yet – 'I don't think I'm the sort of man who kills people.' He'd said it as if owning up to a weakness.

To judge by the sun, lunch came about noon. We stacked up our hoes and walked back to wash our hands under the yard pump. The meal of surprisingly good soup, bread and goat's cheese was served in a room at the front of the house on a line of trestle tables. The princess was there, the first I'd seen of her since our arrival. She sat between Anna and Serafina and her baby in the same black dress and poppy shawl, solicitous that everybody should get his share of the food. She smiled at me occasionally, commented when my plate was empty, but that was all. I wondered if she'd be expecting reports of progress. Veronica sat at the far end of

150

the table, getting up frequently to carry plates to and from the kitchen with remote efficiency, speaking to nobody and without ever a glance at Michael who was sitting near the other end eating nothing and watching her. There was no sign of Glass.

Apart from the princess nobody said much, probably because they were too busy eating. In spite of the frequent assurances of the princess that there was plenty of food, there was a certain amount of silent competition for it. This gave me a chance to look around at the room and the view outside. It was large and high with an ornate plaster ceiling and marble fireplace as souvenirs of the house's grand days. Cobwebs in the corners and blisters on the walls where the lining paper was coming away showed how far the grand days were past. There was no furniture apart from the trestle tables and benches on which we were sitting, no pictures on the wall. Like the state of the kitchen garden it suggested that the commune had been established quite recently. The room was at the front of the house but the view northwards was cut off by another high brick wall. A scrappy lawn, an unkempt gravel drive and rhododendron bushes filled in the gap between wall and house. A secluded place. Even – for an hour perhaps – a defensible place.

The tables were cleared of food, empty plates stacked. As Violet and I were leaving with the others the princess intercepted us.

'The beds are comfortable?'

Yes, we assured her, well versed in the prison tradition of no complaints, no trouble.

'You have enough food?'

She seemed really anxious about it and beamed when we said yes again. I think this horror that anybody should go hungry was the centre of her reforming beliefs, such as they were. Nothing was said about my investigations, which suited me as I hadn't decided how much I wanted to tell her.

I'd expected another spell of weeding, but a wall-eyed man who seemed to act as foreman was waiting for us in the yard to let us know that we'd been assigned a new duty for the afternoon, mucking out the goat house. He led the way into the warm and odiferous darkness, explained how we were to do it and departed. It struck me that we were being deliberately separated from the others and I wondered if a report of my activities that morning had already got to Glass. Violet wrinkled her nose.

'Whiffs a bit, don't it?'

I pointed out that unless we got a change of clothes soon the goats would be the ones with reason to complain. She agreed, and after we'd got the first of the goats into a different pen so that we could sort out its straw, we discussed how to set about it. I suggested approaching Anna since she seemed to be in charge of things on the domestic side.

'You can if you like, but I'm not asking her. Jimmy says not to get too friendly with her.'

I registered that Jimmy Kelly was already becoming an oracle.

'I don't think we should get too friendly with anybody, including Jimmy. We don't know anything about any of them.'

'You don't know anything about anybody until you get to know them.'

Indisputable. She was offended and we worked in silence for a while, until she accidentally launched a forkful of dirty straw down the back of my neck and fished, giggling, to get most of it out again.

This made the question of clean clothes even more clamant, so after we'd finished another loose box to show willing I went to find Anna in the kitchen and put our case. The yard was quiet and deserted, the downstairs corridor equally so. The kitchen door was closed. I tapped on it and heard Anna's voice.

'Who is it? Wait a minute.'

There were scufflings inside. I waited several minutes before Anna opened the door to me, grinning and flushed of face.

'Oh, it's you.'

152

The grin disappeared.

I walked past her into the room. The yeast smell that clung to her was stronger than usual, with a fruity undertone of plum brandy, although she gave no sign of being drunk. There was a man in the kitchen. He was sitting at the kitchen table, big feet bare and splayed, shirt hanging out of his trousers and unbuttoned at the neck to show a mat of dark curling hair, thick as a poodle's coat. He had a cheerful, pudding face and a bushy black beard. He raised a tumbler to me, grinned and said a word that I didn't recognise but took to be a toast. There was dough on the table, pushed aside, amid a dusting of flour. As Anna closed the door I noticed that the back of her green blouse was flour dusted too.

I decided not to apologise and launched instead into a humble request for clothes. She listened with condescension.

'Out you go, Turnip, I've got work to do.'

He went, still cheerful, shambling on his big bare feet, clutching the tumbler. Anna led the way into one of the downstairs rooms – the women's dormitory to judge by the iron bedsteads and the clothes strewn round it – and opened a large wardrobe in the corner full of folded clothes, obviously second-hand but tolerably clean. I sorted out two lots of skirt, blouse, stockings and underwear for Violet and myself while Anna sat on a bed and watched.

'Well, did you dry his tears, then?'

'Whose?'

'You know whose, you were talking to him long enough. About Veronica, I suppose.'

I noticed again her tack-tack way of saying the name.

'You don't like Veronica?'

She made a gesture like somebody flipping away a fly.

'I don't care about her, but she hates me. She'd like to kill me.'

'Why?'

'Because she wants all the men for herself.'

153

I measured stockings against each other, trying to sort out the longest.

'If she'd really wanted to kill you, didn't she have her chance when you were on that cart together?'

'How?'

She looked, for a moment, alarmed.

'Didn't she have a gun?'

'You think I'd go somewhere with that woman if she had a gun? I told Glass, don't give that one a gun unless you want me coming back dead.'

'And he didn't?'

'Of course he didn't.'

'And yet she was on the cart with you. Was that because Withering insisted?'

She smiled, but wouldn't say anything else. When I'd made my choice of clothes she ushered me down the steps to the yard with my arms full and closed the door behind me.

The man she'd called Turnip was sitting on the bottom step, happily hazy, shirt still untucked. I checked that the door was really closed, put my armful on the top step and sat down beside him. Immediately his heavy arm came round my shoulders and he puffed onion and plum brandy breath into my face.

He said something incomprehensible, but obviously friendly, and passed the tumbler to me. I drank cautiously, my ear wedged against his muscular upper arm.

'You're Turnip?'

He recognised the name at least, grinned and nodded. He wanted to know my name and I managed to heave it over the language barrier to him, wishing I knew Russian or Latvian. I tried German, commenting that it was good drink. Success. His grin cracked wider and he replied in German that was clumsy but serviceable. The drink was good drink, Anna was a good woman, I was a good woman too. All the time he had his arm clamped round me and his great throaty chuckles vibrated through me. When he passed me the tumbler again I managed to slide out from under his arm and sit upright, though still close.

While all this was going on, I was weighing up his physique. I'd had only a brief glimpse of the hooded executioner on the cart. He'd been at least an averagely large man, but Turnip struck me as well over the average, in breadth if not in height. It was hard to judge as I'd been at pavement level at the time, but my first impression was that Turnip was not the executioner. The princess thought he was. On the other hand, she hadn't been there. No time or chance for finesse, with Anna just inside and the language limitations. I said, still in German, that Anna had been a very good lion. He seemed to know what I meant. At least he agreed gustily that Anna was a most beautiful lion.

'And you.'

He gave a brandy-flavoured growl and held up his free hand in a claw. He also, a magnificent lion, a strong lion.

'But you weren't a lion, were you?'

Caught in mid-roar he looked troubled, disappointed.

'Were you on the cart?'

He caught at the word, though not my question. A beautiful cart. Glass had made it. Did I know Glass? A clever man at making things.

'Very clever. Did you help him?'

His face fell. No, he hadn't helped. Glass had done it himself, with Anna and the Englishman who died. He seemed sad to have been left out, then his grin came out again.

'But I looked after the horse and made him beautiful. A good horse, a fine horse.'

It had been, I knew, a poor old nag scarcely capable of raising a trot until seriously alarmed.

'You groomed the horse, got him ready?'

He nodded. Now his thoughts had turned to the horse he was crooning to himself about it, making motions with his free hand in the air like a groom using a body brush.

'He loved me, that horse, Peterkin. He would take carrot from my lips, like this.'

155

He pursed them, his eyes staring into mine. Then, as I watched, the expression in them changed from satisfaction to sadness. Two great tears gathered in the corners of his eyes.

'But he didn't come back. Anna and the others came back, but not poor Peterkin. I ask Anna when he's coming back, but she won't tell me.'

If the dynamite plan had worked his Peterkin would have been blown into collops. The driver and the people on the cart could have run away, but not the horse in the shafts. Could Turnip have known that? Even allowing for the fact that his German wasn't good, he didn't strike me as a clever man.

I said, 'I know about Peterkin. He's safe.'

Which was true. He was probably eating better food in the police pound than here. Besides, I thought I owed Turnip that. He'd confirmed what I'd already begun to suspect, that Sophia had been wrong about the identity of the executioner. If Turnip had been one of the four survivors on the cart, he'd know that Peterkin had simply been abandoned in a south London street. In return the heavy arm came thudding round my shoulder again. We both had to drink to Peterkin's health and safety.

Which was all very well except that Turnip's wits, already mazy, were becoming more wandering with every gulp. He was in a state where he'd have told me anything – if only he could have remembered it.

'You were supposed to be the executioner, were you, with an axe and a hood?'

I mimed axe and hood to make sure. He thought about it for a while, then nodded and kept on nodding.

'But you weren't in the end. It was somebody else.'

It took several attempts to get that through to him before the puzzlement in his eyes cleared.

'I'd had a little bit to drink and I wasn't feeling so very good. He wanted to do it, so I thought there'd be no harm, nobody would know. Anna knew, but Anna won't tell anybody else. Anna's a good woman.'

A long rhapsody, in some anatomical detail, about what a very good woman Anna was. I cut it off in its prime.

'Who was he?'

'Who?'

Jolted out of one track, he couldn't find his way back easily.

'The man who was the executioner instead of you?'

'Can't remember his name. Can't remember all their names.'

It was true. He was past being cunning.

'Did he look like this?'

I described Jimmy Kelly as best I could.

'Perhaps, perhaps. He was a good man. He stole a bottle from the kitchen for me. Anna didn't know.'

So somebody, who might have been Jimmy Kelly, had got Turnip drunk – or even drunker than usual – and taken his place. And, by Michael's story, all through that long journey to London the person hadn't taken off his hood or said a word. Wanting certainty, I kept asking Turnip about this other man, what he'd looked like, what he'd sounded like, but couldn't get any sense out of him. In the end he keeled over and went to sleep resting against my shoulder, snoring gustily. It took me a long time to ease him down until he was lying horizontally along the step, mouth open and eyes closed.

Violet was waiting impatiently for the clothes.

'You took your time. I thought you were making them.'

We finished mucking out the goats and decided to change where we were among the bales of straw. Violet sat down on one of the bales, took off her prison stockings and drew on the clean ones with a critical eye on the darns.

'Jimmy Kelly dropped in while you were away.'

'Oh. How did he know where to find you?'

'He knows his way round. I remembered what you said about wanting to know more about him.'

'Yes.'

'He's not like the rest of them here. He says he's a trade unionist. They're not anarchists, apart from some called

157

anarcho-sinners or something like that, and he says there aren't many of those and nobody bothers about them anyway.'

'What's he doing here, then?'

'He had to go somewhere or he'd have been arrested, and a friend of his knew about this place.'

'Arrested?'

'They've got this dock strike up in Liverpool and things got a bit out of hand. It wasn't his fault, but he knew he'd get blamed for it.'

She patted the stocking into place, looking complacently at the curve of her calf.

'Do you know how long he's been here?'

'Not long. He's only waiting here until a friend of his fixes up a ship for him.'

'Ship?'

'Yes. He got a message to this friend who works in the docks. He says he'll fix him up with a ship to Australia.'

This was unwelcome news. I didn't want to lose sight of Jimmy until I'd asked him about his part in events, particularly how his boots came to be scorched.

'The thing is, Nell . . .'

She knotted a piece of binder twine in place of a garter.

'The thing is, he said would I like to go with him.'

'What?'

She misinterpeted my consternation.

'Well, it was you who kept on at me to go. After all, it won't be for a day or two and you might be finished here by then.'

'A day or two! Off to the other side of the world just like that with a man you hardly know!'

'Don't take it like that, Nell. After all, there's not a lot of future for me here, is there? I mean, I can't stay on the run all my life.'

Should I say that I strongly suspected that Jimmy Kelly had been part of the attempt to blow up Scotland Yard? That he might have been the man who shot Withering? I had no proof. Anyway, she'd think I was interfering for my own selfish reasons and take no notice.

158

'Be careful, Violet.'

'Careful? Be nice to have the chance, wouldn't it?'

She secured binder twine round the second stocking in a neat bow.

'That feels like an improvement at any rate. Pity you couldn't do anything about shoes.'

SEVENTEEN

HOW, IN AN ANARCHIST COMMUNITY, do you get people to do the dirty jobs that nobody fancies? In the past I'd heard theoretical anarchists of the lettuce-eating variety debate that for hours on end. The answer was usually moral persuasion. After supper that evening I met it in practice when Violet and I came under strong moral persuasion from Anna to take our turn at the washing up. Whether it was practical necessity or whether she was under orders from Glass to keep us separated from the others I didn't know. Anyway, I resisted it. I'd done enough washing up at Geraldine's coronation ball to last me for several months and I had more urgent things to do. I'd wanted to intercept Veronica after supper, but she'd disappeared. I left Violet up to the elbows in soapy water and went in search of her.

There was no sign of her in the yard. A few of the men were standing around, smoking thin cigarettes that smelt as if they were rolled from lettuce and weeds. I noticed they were looking towards the back gates. There was a beam of wood across the gates, resting on iron brackets screwed into the brickwork on either side, so heavy that it would take two men to lift it. I couldn't remember it there the day before, and when I strolled closer I saw brick dust and a few wood shavings on the ground. The men stared at me and the beam impassively, but they had the air of waiting for something unwanted. The defences were going up. I went back inside to the dimly lit corridor. The gas mantle was hissing and turning blue, but nobody seemed concerned to change it. The door to the women's dormitory was ajar and inside the room a woman was singing a lullaby, with the occasional little gurgling cry from the baby as an accompaniment. It was a sweet singing voice, quite low, and the lullaby was a French one I remembered from a long time ago. The unselfconscious grace of the singing, the beautiful pronunciation, were like fresh air. When I stepped into the room I saw that the singer was Veronica. Somehow it wasn't what I'd expected from her, and yet why shouldn't she have a beautiful voice? Michael had told me she was talented. She was looking down at the baby and didn't see me at first. When she sensed that somebody was there she must have thought it was the mother because she held the baby out to me, still singing, with a smile in her eyes. She saw me, the smile died and the singing stopped.

'I'm sorry.'

Serafina came from behind me and took the child. It curled up to her, nuzzling her breast.

'Goodnight, Serafina.'

Veronica stood up, touched the baby's hair with her fingertips, and walked out. I followed. She went up the stairs, out of the light into half darkness, briskly for the first two or three steps, then slowly. Near the top of the stairs she stopped, leaning over the bannister, head down. In the end I followed and stood two steps below her. Her hands were clasping the bannisters. She was crying.

'If there's anything . . .'

She raised her head and stared at me. I'd expected anger and perhaps she was trying to be angry, but there was nothing left but misery.

'You see, it's Robert's child.'

She said it as if answering a question I hadn't asked, tears streaming down her cheeks. Then she went up another step or two and sat down on the landing, out of reach of the gaslight from below, leaning against the stair rails. I hesitated for a while, then went and sat down a few stairs below, near but not too near, so that she could talk or not talk as she wanted. She wanted to talk. She decided that after a few minutes and by then her voice was calm, although it was too dark to see if she were still crying.

'Robert met Serafina while he was in Italy. She and the baby came back with him.'

'Was she his wife?'

'In the only way that matters.'

'But you and he . . .?'

'Were lovers? Yes.'

'And Serafina didn't mind?'

'Serafina believes as we all do, that men and women have no rights of ownership over each other.'

'Quite true, but they still have feelings.'

'Feelings! Feelings are one of the luxuries of the rich.'

'Was that what Robert Withering said?'

I remembered Michael's ugly story, of how Robert had taken Anna to bed to teach Veronica a lesson in revolutionary politics.

'I'd formed my political views before Robert and I became lovers.'

'What will happen to Serafina and the baby now he's dead?'

'They'll be looked after here.'

'Yes, but how long will here last?'

She didn't answer and I sensed that I was putting into words something she'd hoped not to face. I'd expected hostility from her, expected to dislike her too. Perhaps I should have felt drawn to her for leaving a conventional home to lead her own life, but I'd seen the wreckage that the operation had made of Michael. Hardly her fault, but then there are people who go through life strewing human wreckage and somehow it's never their fault. Still, where I'd expected mutual hostility there was none. Strain and grief had flattened the barriers round her.

'They've put a beam across the back gate. Have you seen it?'

'Across the front door too.'

Her voice was flat, tired.

I said, 'I suppose you're expecting a visit from the police. They'll have worked out by now where the dynamite came from.'

'Yes. He won't let them in.'

'He being Glass?'

She nodded.

'Was it Glass's idea that Robert Withering should take the biggest risk?'

'We all shared the risk.'

'You went with him on that cart knowing it was packed with dynamite?'

'Yes.'

'And Anna knew?'

'Yes.'

'But Michael didn't know.'

'I didn't want him to come with us. I told him not to come with us.'

'But he'd go wherever you were.'

'I've told him I don't want him. I've told him to go away.'

'He might not get the chance now.'

'Is that my fault?'

She wriggled her back against the bannister rails, looking down at me a few stairs below. A dog barked outside and a door slammed in the corridor.

'The princess didn't know about the dynamite either, did she? She thought it was just a piece of revolutionary propaganda.'

'There's a lot she chooses not to know.'

'Which must be convenient if it's her money. What would have happened to Michael at Scotland Yard?'

'What do you mean?'

'I assume the plan was that you and Anna and Robert Withering would jump off and run away at the last moment. Difficult for Michael if he didn't know what the plan was.'

'He'd have gone with me.'

'It was a pretty desperate plan in any case. Was it Glass that made it?'

'Robert too.'

'Yet Robert was the man sitting on the dynamite while Glass was safely at home here. Was it always like that with the two of them?'

The light was too dim to see the look on her face and yet I sensed she didn't like Glass.

'Didn't either of them mind if innocent people were killed?'

'Police aren't innocent.'

'What about the people watching?'

She moved impatiently on the stair.

'We'd have shouted to them to get out of the way. It was just Scotland Yard and the police.'

'I don't know much about dynamite, but I don't think it's that precise.'

We were still a long way from Withering's murder, but I was being taken over by a wish to understand her. Perhaps at the back of my mind was the thought that some ten years before, when I was as young as she was, I might have gone the same way.

'You weren't an anarchist when you came here, were you? You just needed somewhere to live, you and Michael. You were cold and hungry and disappointed and you came here.'

'Disappointed?'

'You'd made your big gesture. You'd run away from home and were trying to live an independent life with a man you thought you loved, only it ended up with a room in Paddington and chilblains.'

They must have been bad ones, too. I'd noticed the scars of them on her hands at supper.

'I suppose Michael's been talking to you.'

'He's a very unhappy man, and still very much in love with you.'

'Does that mean I'm responsible for him? Anyway . . .'

Her voice softened, trailed away.

'Anyway, you're unhappy too?'

Another nod.

'You are allowed to be unhappy, aren't you? After all, you loved Robert Withering and he's dead.'

Even though he'd arrived with another woman and child in tow. Even though he'd hurt her deliberately.

'Yes, I loved him. But more than that, I admired and respected him. I'd seen how ugly the world was for people who aren't rich or powerful. Most people put up with that, make some sort of comfortable nest for themselves inside it. Robert was different. He wanted to tear it apart so that something better could grow.'

'And you wanted to help him – even if it meant killing other people – or getting killed yourself.'

'One person's life doesn't matter.'

'If you really meant that you wouldn't be grieving for Robert Withering.'

She made an odd sound, part groan, part impatience and turned her head away. When she spoke again, still without looking at me, what she said came as a surprise.

'Sophia thinks you're going to find out who killed him.'

'Do you want me to?'

'Is it true about your friend? You really were in prison and escaped?'

'Yes.' I waited for her reaction and when none came tried again. 'If I did find out, would you want to know?'

She thought about it for a while, then nodded.

'Yes, I think I'd want to know, even if I didn't do anything about it. At least I'd want to know why.'

'And you have no idea why?'

She twisted a long strand of hair round her fingers.

'No.'

She didn't sound very certain about it.

'You realise that it was one of the four people on the back of the cart?'

'Yes.'

She was at least more honest or more clear-minded about that than Michael or Anna.

165

'That was Anna, Michael, whoever took Turnip's place – and you.'

'Somebody took Turnip's place. I wondered about that.'

I'd implied another question. She'd avoided it.

'You thought it might not be Turnip at the time?'

'I wondered, but . . . Turnip never says much anyway. I didn't take much notice.'

Just possible. After all, she'd have had plenty of other things to think about.

'Somebody – a man – got Turnip drunk and took his place. Somebody from the commune. Have you any idea who?'

She shook her head. I decided not to mention Jimmy Kelly's name for the moment.

'Let's take the others then. Did you all have guns?'

She shook her head. 'Robert had a gun, I didn't.'

Confirmed by Anna, who disliked her.

'Did you know Michael had a gun?'

An intake of breath. She hadn't known.

'He didn't . . .'

'Shoot Robert Withering? He says he didn't – unless I promise to take you away from here, in which case he'll confess anything.'

'Take me away!'

'An insulting idea, I admit, but the man is desperate.'

'You shouldn't have talked to him about me.'

'Probably not. What about you? Do you think he killed Robert?'

'No. He's not brave enough.'

'And you had no gun, so you couldn't have shot him.'

'Why should I shoot him?'

'Jealousy?'

I thought she was going to get up and walk away. I think she thought so too at first, but she stayed. When she spoke her voice was well under control.

'I suppose Michael's been talking about Anna. Well, I

didn't mind, didn't mind at all. You can only be jealous if you think you own people.'

'What about Anna? Was she jealous of you?'

'If she shot him, it wasn't because of that.'

'If she shot him . . . You think she might have?'

'It follows, doesn't it? If it wasn't Michael and it wasn't me, it has to be one of the other two.'

'Supposing it had been Anna, why would she do it?'

The longest silence yet, then in a voice so low that I hardly heard it: 'Because somebody told her to.'

I'd noticed that when people spoke in that tone of voice at the commune there was one name they had in mind. I whispered it back at her.

'Glass?'

She nodded.

'Would Anna do what he told her?'

'Perhaps, if she wanted to. If he promised her money.'

'I haven't seen much sign of that round here.'

'They're stealing Sophia's rings, him and Anna. Sophia pretends not to notice because she doesn't want to.'

There was a rip of harsh barking from the yard below and shouting. A door opened on the landing near us and the princess looked out, hair done up in a turban, and shouted downstairs.

'What's that? What's happening?'

'Probably a cat as usual.'

Veronica spoke from her sitting position and Sophia jumped to see the two of us there.

'Is it the police coming?'

We stayed where we were, ears strained, until a shout came up from the corridor.

'Only the dog being stupid. Nothing out there.'

Sophia put her hand on her heart and disappeared back behind the door. My sense of time running out had increased with the alarm. Quite soon now, at night or in the earliest hours of the morning, it would be more than a dog's stupidity.

'Anna could have shot him. She'd have had to move

quickly though, to do it then clamber over to pick up the reins when the driver ran away.'

Careless, too, about covering her tracks. She'd been quite happy to tell me that one of the alternative suspects had no gun.

'As for the man who took Turnip's place, if we think Anna could have been acting under Glass's orders, so could he. What you haven't told me is why Glass would want him dead. I thought they were supposed to be friends.'

'Glass says a revolutionary has no friends. He thought Robert was a police informer.'

'Why?'

I decided not to tell her that I'd started out with that view myself.

'He decides everybody's a spy sooner or later. There was a man he killed in Geneva. Robert told me.'

I'd been conscious since the dog began barking, of a thin distressed sound from somewhere downstairs. Veronica was aware of it too, becoming increasingly restless as it rose in volume.

'They've woken the baby up.'

Robert's baby.

'I'm sure Serafina can get it to sleep again.'

I wanted to ask more about the relationship between Glass and Withering, but if she'd been the child's own mother she couldn't have been more anxious.

'I'm the only one who can get him to go to sleep when he's like that. I'll have to go to him.'

She stood up and hurried past me down the stairs. I stayed where I was, wondering how far I believed her. It shouldn't have been complicated by whether I liked her or not, but that came into it too. I'd started out expecting to dislike her quite a lot, but now I'd seen how distressed she was, and how bravely in her way she was trying to cope with it, I felt a kind of grudging respect. Wrong-headed, but not a fool.

Either I was very deep in thought, or he moved with

almost incredible softness across the bare boards of the landing. I think he must have come out of the room next to Sophia's, but I didn't hear the door opening. One minute he wasn't there, the next he was looming above me in the dark. When you're sitting two or three stairs down even a man of his small stature looms. I couldn't help giving a gasp and I knew when he spoke that this had pleased him and put me at a disadvantage from the start.

'I think,' said Glass, 'you'd better come with me.'

EIGHTEEN

I WALKED IN FRONT OF him down the stairs. The men lounging in the corridor stopped talking and pressed themselves back against the wall as we passed. There was nobody in the yard and dusk was collecting round the angles of the outhouses and the brick wings of the dragons on the roof. I didn't have to go with him, there was no force about it. But all I'd managed to find out so far suggested that if anybody had the key to what happened on the cart, it was Glass. If he wanted to talk to me, that suited me because I wanted to talk to him. Or so I told myself. I thought at first that we were making for the vegetable garden but before we got to the archway he turned right along a path between two outhouses, shadowy and damp smelling. He walked with surprising lightness for such a clumsy form, as if his head were a gas balloon buoying up the rest of his body.

'Up here.'

A flight of rough stone steps up to what might once have been a stable boy's quarters. Glass pushed open the door and I followed him. He lit an oil lamp hanging from the wall, showing a room that was as neat as a cell, a plank bed with a thin hessian-covered palliasse and a folded blanket, an old kitchen table, a shelf with a few books. One wall was covered with signboards, professionally lettered in black on a white background, the kind of thing you might see as a price list behind the bar of a public house or a café counter. The first one was headed 'Catechism of a Revolutionary'. The orderly black letters that should have

170

been saying 'Lemonade 3d' or 'Patrons are requested not to consume their own food on the premises' announced instead: 'Everything is moral that contributes to the triumph of the Revolution' and 'The Revolutionary has only one aim: Destruction'. Glass sat on the bed. He didn't invite me to sit down.

'What are you doing?'

I'd had plenty of time to think about what I'd say and decided that, with one exception, I might as well tell the truth. Since I was sure he wouldn't believe me whatever I said, that at least was less complicated than the other options. So I gave him a summary of all that had happened since Saturday, the shooting on the cart, our arrests, the two sessions of questioning by the police. He stared up at me, unblinking. When I mentioned the name of Brust, his eyes narrowed. The one point where I deviated from the truth was on the question of Violet. I let it be known that the escape from Holloway was my idea and that I was annoyed because she'd seen an opportunity and tagged along. I tried to make her seem as small a threat to him as I could, practically simple minded. Another of his lip twists, meant as a sardonic grin. It looked as if he'd learned it from an imperfect diagram.

'I know that's the story you told Sophia, but I'm not as stupid as she is. They must have wanted to spy on me very much, to go to all this trouble.'

I'd never been in any doubt that he'd see me as a spy. Even a rational person might have thought so in the circumstances, let alone a man obsessed.

'Do you think they'd have waited until now to send a spy in?'

'Meaning?'

'There was somebody else, wasn't there, long before I got here?'

I watched his face and saw him blink for the first time that I'd noticed. There was a kind of greed there too, as if the idea of being spied on fed something deep inside him. Tired of standing and looking down at him I moved

171

towards his desk, intending to draw out the wooden chair from underneath it. He jumped up.

'Don't move. Stay where you are.'

I gave him a look, pulled the chair out and sat down to face him and the orderly panels of the revolutionary catechism on the wall. 'The Central Committee of the Secret Society should regard all the other members as expendable revolutionary capital.'

I studied it. 'Sergei Nechayev, isn't it? I think he must have been the nastiest person who ever called himself an anarchist. Did your father know him?'

I hadn't set out intending to annoy him, but since things could hardly be worse there seemed no good reason why not. I hate it when people try to intimidate me, particularly when there's a tightness in my chest that suggests they might be succeeding.

He stood a few feet away from me.

'How would you know about other spies here if you're not one yourself?'

To deny it would be a waste of breath. Since nothing in the world would convince him that I wasn't a police spy, I'd use it. I tried not to think about the man in Geneva.

'You must have known about that, didn't you?'

I could see a struggle on his face. He hated admitting ignorance of anything but he was greedy for what he thought I could tell him.

'Did Brust tell you he had another spy here?'

'He didn't tell me anything, but what would you do in his place?'

'Sophia makes it easy for them, letting in anybody with a hard-luck story, like you.'

'Robert Withering didn't come with a hard-luck story, did he? He came as a revolutionary.'

'She doesn't know anything about revolutionaries. Sophia's as riddled with class consciousness as a rotting carcase with maggots. She'll roll over on her back for anything that's got the stink of the ruling classes about it, like he had.'

172

'And, of course, Withering was very handsome.'

I'd never seen young Withering alive but I had Geraldine's opinion that he was attractive. Anyway, most men would seem handsome in comparison to Glass.

'It wasn't only the princess he impressed, was it? There was Veronica as well.'

'A revolutionary has no business with women. He has no affairs, no sentiments, no attachments.'

Most of that was in the catechism on the wall behind him. He quoted it without having to turn round to look.

'Apparently Robert Withering didn't agree.'

'Robert Withering was not a revolutionary.'

He stared at me. I stared back.

'What was he, then?'

'You know what he was.'

'A spy, you mean?'

He didn't answer, but a kind of glow came over his face.

'Was that why you had him shot?'

'It's what happens to spies.'

There I had it, for all the good it would do me. Robert Withering had been shot on Glass's orders either by Anna or the man who'd taken Turnip's place, ostensibly for being a police spy, probably through envy. There were only three problems. Firstly, I had no proof. Secondly, I couldn't get out of the place. Thirdly, it was too easy. Glass was virtually insane with spy mania.

My eyes fell on an appropriate passage on one of the lettered boards on the wall. I read it out.

' "We recognise no other authority but the work of extermination, poison, the knife, the rope etcetera. In this struggle revolution sanctifies everything." '

'I did it myself. In my employer's time.'

'Poisoning and so on?'

'Sign painting. My trade. I worked for a brewery in Wolverhampton. Lettering first, then they graciously let me do the pub signs and paid me two bob a week more. Talented, they said I was. I was laughing at them all the time. In the front of the workshop when the manager came

round, there were all the signs to cheat the workers out
of their money, Duke of Clarence, Queen Victoria, Lord
Nelson. In the back I had this – with their brushes and
their paint. Like the revolution undermining them all the
time they were guzzling.'

'I suppose they found out and sacked you.'

Setting off, in the process, a career that would go on to
trying to blow up Scotland Yard. I'd never look at a pub
sign in quite the same light again – always supposing I saw
one again.

'They didn't find out. I made a gesture.'

'What kind of gesture?'

'They were opening a new place, a grand opening with
all the directors there. They said they wanted me to do a
sign for it that would really make people stop and open their
eyes. The pub was the King's Head. I did this.'

He stood up and pulled out a board from under his bed. It
would have been a break with tradition in any case to make
a pub sign out of his late majesty King Edward VII complete
with bald dome and pointed beard. To do it the way Glass
had done it, head hacked off at the neck and dripping gouts
of blood, eyes staring aghast, would put anyone off his beer.
He propped it against the wall and stared at it with gloomy
pride. There was a little dark patch clinging to the top of
the king's bald head, a dead moth probably. He brushed
it off, staring lovingly at the picture.

'I installed it myself and kept it covered up. The chair-
man's wife did the unveiling.'

'Did she appreciate it?'

His whole body began to quiver, quite silently, as if
something were agitating the filaments that propel fungi
underground. It took me a while to realise that he was
laughing.

'Appreciate. I like that. She appreciated it all right.
Fainted right there and then in the road. Then they went
and arrested me for disturbing the peace.'

'And you went on to greater things, like trying to blow
up Scotland Yard. Only you failed. What went wrong?'

The laugh cut off abruptly.

'No business of yours.'

'If you'd decided to have Robert Withering shot, wouldn't it have been better to have it done after they'd delivered the dynamite to Scotland Yard and were running off?'

With Withering's body left in the rubble. That would have appealed to him.

'But something went wrong, didn't it? The whole thing nearly went up while they were on the bridge. Did your man panic? Or was it woman?'

'What happened on the bridge?'

'I'd have thought you knew. Surely they reported back to you.'

'Not your business. Tell me.'

'The draperies were burning. The man in the king's head – Withering – and the executioner seemed to be trying to stamp them out. I suppose they were worried the whole thing would go up with them on it.'

'Did he look drunk?'

'Withering? No.'

'The other one.'

I had to turn away in case my excitement showed. Turnip was a notorious drunk. Turnip was supposed to be the man under the executioner's hood. I knew that he wasn't. Was it credible that Glass didn't know? But then, who would have told him? Not Turnip, certainly. Not Michael and probably not Veronica, who disliked Glass. That left only one person likely to have told him: Anna. She'd have known, but from what I'd seen in the kitchen she had a liking for Turnip, to put it mildly. It was possible at any rate that she might be protecting him from his dereliction of duty.

'Not drunk as far as I could see. But it would be hard to tell. Why did you choose Turnip anyway? You must have known he drank. Or was he the one who'd be stupid enough to stay on the cart till the end?'

Almost sure now that he really didn't know what had happened, I was deliberately trying to annoy him into another mistake. I looked at his face and realised I'd overdone it. He was standing up, fist on his desk, staring at me with the look of a boil about to burst. I measured the distance to the door.

'How did you know it was Turnip? What is it to you anyway?'

His hand went into the desk drawer and came out holding a revolver. He pointed it at me.

'You know what we do to spies.'

In retrospect, I'm almost certain he had no intention of shooting me there and then, not while he thought I had information he needed. I'd been gambling on that all along. But retrospect's a nice comfortable grandstand and it wasn't where I was sitting at the time. He was pointing the gun at me and his aim looked steady. When I stood up the angle of the gun moved with me. I took a step towards the door and it shifted again.

'You'll have some explaining to do to Sophia.'

'Damn Sophia. I don't explain to anyone.'

I ducked down, intending to make a dive for the door and saw in the lamplight the melancholy detruncated head of his late majesty staring at me. I grabbed it, with some idea I think of using it as a shield. It was after all a stout pub sign, not a flimsy canvas.

'You leave that alone.'

He might have been a royalist protesting at lese-majesty. I straightened up, arms almost buckling under the weight of the thing but all that exercise on Hampstead Heath with Indian clubs came in useful at last and, with force and follow-through that did my heart good to feel it, brought the sign down firmly on the top of his head. He went down like a dead branch cracking, with an explosion that vibrated round and round the room. The revolver must have gone off as he fell. The bullet from it went goodness knows where, but at least nowhere near me.

It took me a few seconds to realise that, what with the noise and the shocking effectiveness of me and my royal ally. In those few seconds, as the sound waves died away enough to make thinking possible, I heard feet pounding up the steps outside, then a man's voice, low but urgent.

'What's happening in there?'

A voice with traces of Yorkshire in it. Digby's voice. I took a couple of shaky steps and opened the door to him.

He walked in, looked at Glass on the floor then at me.

'Have you killed him?'

I knelt down beside Glass. He moved his head feebly from side to side and opened his mouth.

'No.'

'That's a pity.' He had his pipe out of his pocket, rubbing the bowl of it. 'But then I suppose you wouldn't have liked to.'

'You were outside?'

In spite of what he'd said, I had the idea that Digby was only the advance guard of a tribe of avengers, that Glass's supporters would come rushing in from all sides. I wanted to get away but Digby was between me and the door and for the moment I had no strength left to do anything about it.

'I'd followed you, in case you needed a bit of help.'

The consciousness that he might be an ally was beginning to break through my shock, but I was still expecting other feet on the stairs, shouts. They didn't come.

'He was pointing a gun at me.'

'That one?'

It was on the floor. Digby picked it up, checked it and laid it down carefully on the desk. He did it like a man who was used to handling firearms.

'What will happen now? People will have heard the shot. Won't they come and . . .?'

He shook his head.

'They see you going off with him, they hear a shot. They'll stay out of it if they've got any sense.'

'You mean, they'll think he was shooting me?'

He nodded. I felt, if anything, shakier to think that nobody in the place would have dared to intervene – except Digby, and he'd have been too late.

'I should thank you.'

177

On the floor, Glass stirred and groaned.

'Time to go.'

I'd been comforted by Digby's air of solid calm the first time I met him, even more so now. Glad for once to let somebody else do the thinking I followed him down the steps to the alleyway, then through the arch into the dark vegetable garden. There was no sign of anybody. Only a dog gave a few barks then went quiet. We stopped by the far wall and the sharp tang of mint rose round us, from the plants our feet were crushing. Digby lit his pipe, politely asking my permission first, and neither of us said anything else until he'd taken a few drags on it.

'Could you manage to get over the wall if I helped you?'

'Yes, but . . . I'm not going yet. There's my friend here and things I've still got to do.'

That talk with Glass that should have answered questions had only raised more. Glass himself didn't know there'd been a substitute for Turnip on the cart. It followed that if that substitute had shot Withering, he wasn't acting on Glass's orders. I still didn't know why Withering had been killed and without that I couldn't expect Brust or anybody else to believe me. I offered to help Digby over the wall if he liked. I could tell he didn't fit in there and he might be in worse trouble for helping me.

'Nowhere to go. Stay here till the bitter end, I have to.'

There was nothing self-pitying about the way he said it, only an immense sadness. I wondered what he could have done in the outside world to keep him here. His familiarity with guns and sense of order suggested some military background.

'Why?'

The pipe made whistling sounds, drawing in air as the tobacco burnt out. It was good smelling tobacco too, not like the cigarettes the other men smoked. I remembered how carefully he was rationing it out to himself in half wafers. A link with something lost.

'You live your life the way you think's right, doing your duty, serving your country. Then you make one mistake

178

and that's it. Doesn't matter why you did it because nobody wants to hear. You've made your mistake and there's no way back, and that's all there is to it.'

I thought of the shined boots.

'Were you in the army?'

He nodded. I wondered what the one mistake could be, so fatal that it turned a dutiful soldier into an outcast among anarchists. Striking an officer? Killing a comrade? It might have happened not long ago, since he'd been in touch with the outside world recently enough to have his little store of good tobacco.

Something white brushed against my face. Nerves over-stretched, I put up my hand, gasped.

'You're not scared of a moth, are you?'

He was laughing. Something moved in my head.

'Not a moth. It wasn't a moth.'

He was staring at me, match in hand, alarmed. From his point of view I was talking nonsense because it had indisputably been a moth that brushed my face.

'Not that one. The one on his signboard. I thought it was a squashed moth, but it wasn't. It was a piece of your tobacco.'

Half a wafer of it, stuck to the king's bald head. The match went out. After the glare I couldn't see his face.

'I wondered what became of that. Did he notice?'

'I don't think so. How did it get there? Were you searching his room?'

He didn't answer directly, seeming more concerned to defend himself against untidiness.

'Seeing that thing shocked me. If you're loyal, it shocks you what people can do. I went for this.' His arm moved, gesturing with the pipe. 'Then I thought, no, he'd smell the smoke when he got back, so I put it back in my pocket. Only I couldn't see what I'd done with the tobacco.'

'What are you trying to do?'

'Same as you are, only I'm in it deeper. They didn't have to send you, you know. It only makes it worse if I have to look after you as well.'

'You don't have to look after me.'

After all, I was the one who'd floored Glass, not him. Still, it was no more than a routine protest. I was more concerned who 'they' were. If I asked him it would only prove that I knew less than he thought. I needed time to work out what I knew and half knew.

'I think I'll go in, if you don't mind.'

There'd been no hue and cry on Glass's behalf. It was possible that he hadn't come round yet and I supposed, in bare humanity, that I'd have to find an excuse for sending somebody to find him. He might not even admit what had happened. It would be humiliating for a man so prone to brooding on ropes and guns to confess that he'd been felled by his own artistic work.

'Yes.'

Digby sounded as if he were worrying about something, trying to make up his mind. As I turned to go he said:

'When you go, will you take a letter out for me?'

'Yes, of course. If I go before you do.'

'Oh, you'll do that all right.'

I was conscious again of the sadness in his voice.

'Good-night, Digby. And thank you.'

For what I wasn't sure, but I still hoped and thought he meant well. He wished me good-night, not using my name, and I left him standing there on the mint under the wall.

NINETEEN

THERE WERE STILL A FEW men in the downstairs corridor,
some of them sitting on the floor, legs bent, backs against
the wall. The kitchen door was ajar and as I passed it I
saw Anna with Turnip and two other men playing cards
at the table by candlelight. I looked in.

'I think Mr Glass may need some help.'

From the look on their faces I was supposed to be the
one who needed help.

'Why? What's happened?'

'He's hit his head on something.'

I left them staring at each other, apparently in no great
hurry to do anything, and went downstairs to our room
in the basement. It was in darkness. I groped for matches
and a candle stub that produced a dim light but there was
no sign of Violet. This worried me as it seemed very late
at night, but the day had started early so perhaps my time
sense was adrift. I wondered if she'd managed to get away
after all. At one time I'd have been pleased about that, but
now it would mean she'd gone with Jimmy Kelly.

It was some time before it struck me that the rats were
being noisier than usual next door. I'd got used to their
squeaks and scufflings the night before, but now they
sounded the size of puppies. There were muffled thumps,
a rustling sound, then a squeal remarkably like a person
giggling. I tried to ignore them and grapple with the
problem of what to do next, then there was another
squeal. I picked up my candle stub and an old chair leg
that was lying around and advanced next door to establish

181

some peace and quiet. When I flung the door open the shadows wavering on the wall in the candlelight made me think at first that I'd found king rat from a pantomime. Then they turned into two human figures and my eyes followed them down to see Violet and Jimmy sitting on a pile of old sacks, side by side.

'Hello, Nell.'

'I'm sorry, I didn't mean to . . .'

'Don't worry, we were just talking, weren't we Jimmy?'

He was slower, perhaps worried by the sight of me with a chair leg in hand, but his grin broke through and he followed her lead.

'Yes, Violet was telling me all about you, what you're doing here.'

I gave Violet a look. Too late, now the damage was done, but that meant Jimmy Kelly was forewarned. Nothing now except direct attack, but I'd have to warn her. I asked if we could have a word and she followed me reluctantly next door, leaving Jimmy sitting on the sacks in darkness. No way to sugar the pill.

'Violet, you have to know. I'm nearly sure Jimmy's the man I'm looking for.'

'Yes, I think he's the man I've been looking for too.'

In spite of the surroundings she seemed as blithe as a schoolgirl on a picnic, still inclined to giggle.

'He took somebody else's place on the cart and shot Robert Withering. I don't know why yet, I think some kind of anarchist feud but . . .'

'No he didn't, Nell.' She was shaking her head, trying to be patient with me. 'He doesn't know anything about the cart or the Withering man.'

'Did you ask him how his boots came to be burnt?'

'I'm sorry, Nell, but we've had more important things to talk about than his bloody boots.'

She was becoming annoyed and so was I.

'Has he told you anything about what he was doing before he came here?'

'A bit, but that doesn't matter any more. It will all be

different when we get out to Australia, new start for both of us.'

'Violet, you can't get away from the past just like that. If somebody's . . .'

I was going to say that a man ruthless enough to commit a murder on the instructions of a lunatic like Glass wouldn't change simply by sailing to the other side of the world. But before I could finish her eyes were flashing fury. I'd never seen her so angry, not even with the other women in the police station.

'You bitch, Nell. I'd never have thought you'd have been so cheap, you of all people.'

'For goodness' sake, what have I said?'

'Throwing my past up at me like that. Well, you needn't worry because I told him about it as soon as I knew I'd started liking him. I told him and he doesn't bloody care.'

Light dawned, and with it a rush of pity for her and anger at my clumsiness. I was so preoccupied with Jimmy that I'd forgotten the interpretation she might put on what I said.

'Oh God, I'm sorry. Nothing could have been further from my mind. It was *his* past I was thinking about.'

'Do you think I mind if he got into a bit of trouble with the police trying to stand up for himself? Was he supposed to see his friends knocked about and their families starving and not do anything about it?'

It took some time to calm her down, longer to convince her that I had to ask Jimmy Kelly some questions, whether she liked it or not. Even then she insisted on going back next door with me. The wavering remains of our candle revealed Jimmy still sitting on his pile of sacks, looking quite happy.

'Made it up then have we, ladies?'

Not surprising that he'd heard Violet's raised voice from next door.

I said, 'Violet's angry with me because I want to ask you some questions.'

183

'Ask away.'

I put the candle stub on a rusted upturned bucket and sat down on some sacks facing him. Violet stood by the door, watching me.

'She's told you I'm interested in the cart and Withering being shot?'

'That's right.'

'There were four people on the back of it besides Withering. Three of them might have shot him, the other one didn't have a gun. One of the four was supposed to be a man named Turnip. You know the man I mean?'

He nodded and made a lifting motion with his elbow, parodied by the shadow on the wall behind him.

'On Saturday somebody got him very drunk and took his place. Turnip's quite broad-shouldered, so it would have to be a man of at least average size.'

I thought of his bare chest as he splashed in the water trough, glanced at Violet and suspected she was thinking of it too. Jimmy Kelly said nothing.

'When they got to Westminster Bridge something went wrong. Perhaps the person who was supposed to be lighting the fuse was nervous and dropped the match. Anyway, the draperies caught fire and it looked as if the whole cart would go up too early, with them on it. The man who'd taken Turnip's place acted very quickly and bravely. He stamped out the fire.'

'Whoever he was, he had some nerve.'

Jimmy's eyes were on me, apparently absorbed in the story.

'He certainly had, because I think within a few seconds of that he pulled out a gun and shot Robert Withering dead. Perhaps he blamed him for starting the fire, but I think it went back further than that.'

'Then what?'

'All four of them got away and found themselves back here. So whoever that man was, he's still here now.'

Violet tried to break in with a warning. 'Jimmy, what she's trying . . .'

He held up a hand and she went quiet.

'So who is he?'

'His boots would be burnt, stamping out the fire.'

I picked up the candle stub suddenly and held it close to his boots. They were covered with dust and the dead leaves of weeds, but there was one deep burn mark on the toe of the right boot, easily visible.

'Like that.'

He took a long breath.

'So that's it, is it?'

The candle was almost out, nothing more than a smear of hot wax, burning my fingers. The wick chose that moment to fall sideways and I dropped it on the floor, stamping it out. In the shock of the complete darkness I heard Violet's voice.

'There was another one under the sacks where Jimmy's sitting. I reckon this is where they store the candles.'

Jimmy Kelly's fingers and mine scrabbled under the sacks and met, accidentally curled round each other, drew apart. Then mine closed on what we wanted.

'Here we are. Has anybody got a match?'

Nobody had, but I remembered there were some next door in our room. We jostled in the doorway and I thought that any hope of catching Jimmy Kelly off balance had gone for good. Since I'd just virtually accused him of murder it was in my mind that he might attack me, but there was simply nothing to be done about it. For a few scrabbling minutes in the mouldy darkness we were just three creatures blundering against each other, trying to find light. In the end we got ourselves into the room next door and my fingers closed on the matchbox. Needing both hands to strike the match I passed the candle to the person closest to me – Violet, by the feel of the fingers. The match flared.

Dazzled by the light, I looked for a wick.

'Hold on a minute, it's all wrapped up. I'd better . . .'

A blue-paper covered cylinder in her hand, larger than I'd expected. A smell that wasn't wax. Marzipan smell.

'Violet, put that down.'

'Make up your mind, Nell. I'm just trying . . .'

'PUT IT DOWN.'

Jimmy, who'd caught the alarm in my voice before she did, grabbed it from her. I crushed the match out between my palms, not even feeling the pain. From the restored darkness, Violet protested.

'What's come over you two? What's happening?'

We hustled her out into the corridor, bumping and gasping through a maze of dark passages and rooms until we were sitting on the stone steps leading up to the rest of the house. Violet was almost breathless by then, but still gulping out demands for an explanation. Jimmy gave it.

'It wasn't a candle you'd got hold of. It was dynamite.'

She gave a little scream. Her hand brushed mine, clutched it.

'What was dynamite doing down there?'

I said to Jimmy Kelly, 'Do you know?'

His reply came down from the top of the steps.

'No. No more than I know who shot your man on the cart.'

Violet wasn't concerned with that.

'Why are we sitting here talking about it? Let's get out before it all blows up.'

Now that I'd calmed down a little and had a chance to remember some of the few things I knew about the behaviour of dynamite, this didn't seem quite so likely. Still, I shared her view that there were more salubrious places.

'We'd better not tell anybody. If there's anybody in the passage, just walk out casually into the yard.'

'Just listen to her – casually! Go like bloody greyhounds.'

Still she managed to walk calmly enough along the ground floor passageway. Anna, still sitting with her card school in the kitchen, watched sardonically as the three of us filed past the door but said nothing. Outside, Violet drew a deep breath.

'Right, that's it. I'm getting out of here.'

Jimmy said quietly, 'That might not be so easy.'

He was looking where I was looking, towards the back gates. A lamp had been hooked to the gatepost and by its light we could see two men, lounging but watching us. The big beam of wood was in place to hold the gates shut.

'We'll see about that.'

She walked determinedly up to the men on the gate. Jimmy and I looked at each other and followed.

'Open sesame.'

Her voice was jaunty, but with a little tremor in it. They gaped at her.

'I fancy going out for a little stroll.'

One of them looked as if he didn't understand English and the other was obviously taken aback by Violet. He gestured at the heavy beam.

'Two big strong gentlemen like you could lift that for a lady, couldn't you?'

He looked at the ground and mumbled his reply. I caught the word 'Glass'.

'You locking us up here then, like in a prison?'

She was still trying hard, but the tremor was more pronounced.

As she turned away from them, head bent, I remembered her horror of prisons. Jimmy's arm went round her shoulders and he guided her back across the yard.

'It will be all right. We'll get out tomorrow.'

'It'll be too late tomorrow. This place could go up tonight like Crystal Palace. There might be stacks of bloody dynamite down there for all you know.'

I thought she was probably right, and so did Jimmy from the look he gave me. A reluctant kind of alliance was developing between the two of us.

'I don't think it's meant to go up tonight,' I said. 'As far as I remember, dynamite's quite stable. It will only explode if you light a fuse.'

There were probably fuses down there, though, a cats' cradle of them linking room to room through the basement. Glass was expecting the police to come and when they did it wouldn't be Sidney Street all over again. This time the anarchists and their invaders would go up together in one cataclysmic explosion.

'Well, I'm not going back in that house.'

So we decided to go back to the goat house, shushing the welcoming bleats of goats who thought it was feeding time again. We perched in the dark on the straw bales. Violet was still furious.

'They've got no right to keep us here.'

'Well, we can't call a policeman, can we?'

I couldn't see, but I thought Jimmy still had his arm round her. I said, in his direction, 'Did you know what Glass was planning?'

'I didn't and I still don't. The less I have to do with that one, the better.'

I believed him, at least as far as the dynamite in the cellars was concerned. I thought Jimmy Kelly had strong nerves, but they'd have needed to be superhuman for him to sit on a stack of dynamite and watch Violet and me fumbling with candles and matches.

'I suppose you're still worrying about how my boots got burnt.'

'Yes. Yes, I am.'

'Listen to them. We're shut up in this bloody madhouse, blown sky high the minute somebody drops a match and they're still going on about boots.'

He made calming noises to her, much as we'd been making them to the goats, usually an intolerably patronising thing from one human being to another, not in this case. Somehow it made me see, as nothing else did, the closeness between them.

'You see, Violet love, I didn't tell you quite everything I've been doing.'

My heart jumped, thinking he was going to confess, then sank for her.

'You said you had. The police and so on, the fight, you told me you had . . .'

A rustling of straw. I guessed she'd drawn away from his

188

arm and imagined her sitting bolt upright, the way she'd been while waiting for the prison van.

'Just listen. There was one thing I didn't tell you because I thought it might upset you, but now she's asked about it, it might as well come out so that you know the worst. Right?'

She said nothing.

'I told you about the dock strike, and the way the police were in league with the bosses, breaking up our meetings and so on. What I didn't tell you was what we and a few others did about it.'

'What did you do?'

'There was this warehouse in Liverpool, full of cotton stuff. It belonged to one of the men who was trying to starve us out. We got in there one night and set fire to it. What happened was, we'd poured in the paraffin and lit it, then somebody said there might be a night watchman in there, so I had to go in and have a look. There wasn't, but some of the stuff had fallen across the door, so I had to kick it aside to get out. That's how my boots got burnt.'

Violet's long sigh came out of the darkness.

'Oh, is that all?'

'All?' He sounded quite hurt. 'All, she says. It's arson, my love. You can get a life sentence for it. That's why I had to get out of the Pool in a hurry when I knew they were looking for me. How I ended up here.'

More rustling. Violet moving back again. He chuckled like a warm chicken on its nest and I imagined his arm going round her again. When she spoke her voice came from the same direction as his.

'All right then, Nell? Got what you wanted to know?'

I had something, but not what I'd wanted or expected.

'And you say you weren't on that cart?'

'I couldn't have been, not if it happened on the Saturday. I didn't get here till the Sunday. I know it was a Sunday because I'd spent the night before in a church and I had to get out in a hurry in the morning when the women came to put out the hymn books.'

189

'What church?'

'No idea, except it was up on a hill somewhere. I was trying to find my way here. I'd heard from some bloke that they gave you a roof over your head and didn't ask questions, then I walk into all this.'

'So how did you find your way?'

'I had a bit of luck. At least, I thought it was luck at the time. I'd got to Muswell Hill and I was walking around wondering where to try next when I saw this respectable-looking man walking along on his own. So I went up to him and said, politely like, did he know anywhere round here that took in working men down on their luck. He looks at me, says come with me and takes me straight here. It turns out he came from here, the one they call Digby – you know, always looks as if he's on parade.'

'You met Digby on Sunday morning and he brought you here?'

'That's right. You can ask him if you like. He seems quite a sensible bloke – by the standards of this place.'

Jimmy sounded his old self, relaxed and reasonable. I sat there in the wreckage of my last theory and wondered where to go next. I'd set too much store by the burnt boots. I supposed if I were determined to cling to it I might suspect that Digby and Jimmy were in collusion to set up an alibi, but why go to such trouble when I was in no position to do them harm? For the sake of completeness, I would ask Digby when I got the chance, but without much hope. I thought Jimmy was telling the truth.

'Happy then, Nell?'

Violet was recovering too, getting back some of her jauntiness.

'Tired.'

I was too, suddenly, bludgeoningly tired.

'Me too. We'll all try to get a bit of sleep, then as soon as it's daylight we get out of this bloody place if we have to dig a tunnel under the wall.'

Even if we managed it, which I thought unlikely, I'd go with no idea who killed Robert Withering and why. I knew

190

enough, perhaps, to unsettle the police theory of Simon's guilt – but that would depend on their believing me, which was unlikely. We pushed straw bales close together to make a kind of a bed, lay down side by side in our clothes. I'd have given almost anything for clean sheets again, sheets you could pull up over your head and hide under. But I slept, sheets or no sheets, until we were woken by the metallic clamour in the yard to get up and work.

TWENTY

THE ODD THING ABOUT THAT last morning was that we really
did work. Violet, Jimmy and I had a hasty consultation in
the goat house before joining the others and decided that
the best chance of escape would be during the midday or
evening meal. Food was taken seriously in this place where
there wasn't quite enough of it, and there would be fewer
people than usual in the grounds. Although I said nothing
about it to Violet, I still hadn't decided whether to go with
them. She and I joined the queue at the pump together,
leaving Jimmy to follow a few minutes later. It was a shorter
queue than usual and I noticed that most of the men were
hollow-eyed and restless. There was no sign of Glass. When
I saw Anna I wondered whether to ask after his health, saw
the look she gave me and decided against it.

Weeding in the vegetable patch went on, though with
fewer people than usual. I supposed the rota of guard
duties was taking its toll. Even those who were working
didn't have their hearts in it and struck out carelessly with
their hoes, breaking the bright skins of onions so that the
scent of them rose into the warming air and made our eyes
water. A voice spoke in my ear.

'If they thought they were going to be here to eat them,
they wouldn't be hacking at them like that.'

Digby, empty pipe in mouth.

'When are you going?'

'Soon, I think.'

'Soon as you can. Thought of how you're doing it?'

I didn't answer. That seemed to please him.

'That's right. Don't say anything you don't have to. I might be able to give you a bit of help though, if you were to ask me this evening.'

I looked round. As far as I could see there was nobody within earshot, although Anna was watching us as usual.

'You can give me a bit of help now. Tell me something.'

'What?'

'Last Sunday morning you were walking round outside. Remember that?'

He didn't reply. Don't say anything you don't have to. I bent to pull up a pimpernel plant that had wrapped itself round a particularly promising onion.

'Did you meet anybody?'

I heard the air whistling through his empty pipe as he sucked on it, then:

'Yes, I did.'

'Was it somebody who asked you for directions?'

'Yes, it was.'

'Who?'

I thought he wasn't going to reply then, when I looked up at him, I saw he was pointing with his pipe, held down at his side.

'Jimmy Kelly?'

'The Scouser. That's right.'

'So he didn't arrive here until Sunday?'

'That's right. He said he was in a bit of trouble – like all the rest of them.'

His voice was scornful. Soon after that he moved away from me.

'I'll see you later.'

Lunchtime came. I remember that it was mostly potato salad, with a tasty dressing of dill and vinegar. Still no sign of Glass but Veronica was there and the princess presided. She began by trying to be cheerful, but her bright little eyes were sunken and she kept nervously rearranging the fringes of her shawl, glancing from face to face for the reassurance that didn't come. As she was slicing a pallidly gleaming jam

193

suet pudding, as carefully as if our survival depended on the equal division of it, a bell started ringing.

It was a handbell, like the ones that bring schoolchildren in from playtime, but swung with ferocious urgency somewhere in one of the front upstairs rooms, followed by distant shouting. The shouting was taken up from nearer at hand in the yard.

'Police. It's the police.'

Sophia dropped the knife and put her hand on her heart. Most of the men round the table stood up, staring at each other, and for a few seconds nobody moved. Then feet came running downstairs and along the corridor, the bell clanging in time with them. A man burst into the room.

'They're coming. Coming up the path.'

'Where's Glass?'

That came from Sophia, hardly more than a gasp.

'Up there. He says we're to barricade the front door and watch the back gate.'

There was a stampede for the door. The man with the bell followed it, still clanging, leaving only the women in the room. Serafina had grabbed the baby to her and was looking from face to face, terrified. Veronica was as pale as paper but moved to put an arm round her.

'We'll look after you. Don't worry, we'll look after you.'

I went out into the corridor and saw that heavy furniture, a chest of drawers, old armchairs, was being manhandled towards the front door to make a barricade. On my way up the stairs I passed Digby who was leaning on the bannisters watching them.

'Looks like you left it too late, didn't you?'

A pessimist justified. His pipe was going, puffing out clouds of ripe smoke from another world. That scared me more than the bell because it meant he wasn't trying to economise on tobacco any more. I went past him to the upstairs landing and saw that the door to the princess's room was open. The room inside was like a disorderly cave, heavy curtains shutting out most of the daylight, a big sagging bed covered with shawls and draperies, a samovar on a table with spoons and saucers round it. Several men were standing close to the window, clustered round Glass. An argument was going on, low-toned but passionate, so they didn't notice me. As I took a few steps nearer I saw that Glass was holding the gun he'd threatened me with the night before. Even though he was arguing, his eyes were fixed on the gap in the curtains and his clumsy body was as taut as a hound's the moment before it gives tongue.

I moved to the far side of the wide window. If anybody had noticed me by now they had more serious things to think about. When I knelt on the floorboards and moved the curtain aside a fraction I had the view from the front of the house. It was an ordinary enough view. The high brick wall shut off most of it apart from some sky and a few trees and chimney pots. A path of dingy gravel ran from a narrow gate in the wall, presumably towards the front door just below us, between neglected lawns with dark islands of rhodondendron and sprawls of pink roses. Even the policemen hesitating half-way down the drive looked ordinary. There were just two of them, one tall and thin, one of average size. The average-sized one was looking up at the window and saying something. He had a clean-shaven face, very pink, as if he'd been recently in the sun. As far as I could see, they were both constables. The taller one said something in reply, then they both began to move slowly towards the front door. The argument going on round Glass rose in pitch, until he took his attention off the path for a moment and snarled at them to be quiet. He didn't quite threaten them with the gun, just altered the angle of it a fraction, but it was enough. The room went so quiet that we could hear the crunching of the policemen's steps below on the gravel, then the steps coming to a halt. When the knock came on the door it sounded thunderous, echoing through the half-furnished house. Glass drew in his breath with a hissing sound. Silence for a while, then the shifting of feet on the gravel. We heard, quite clearly, one policeman telling the other to try again. Another knocking, more thunderous than before. This time the silence following it was broken by feet scuttling up the stairs and the princess's voice:

'What's happening?'

Glass said, without turning his attention from the window, 'Keep her out.'

But nobody moved and the princess came running in. She went towards the group at the window, still demanding to know what was happening. Glass swore at her over his shoulder and she came to halt a few yards away from him. When she noticed me she gave me an appealing look, but I wasn't moving either.

Another knock, going on and on this time. Then one of the policemen said to the other, 'I don't think they're going to answer.'

More steps on the gravel then both policemen came into view again as they drew back from the front door to take a look at the house. They were looking up towards our window, but I don't know if they'd seen us behind the curtains. The tall one cupped a hand round his mouth and shouted, 'Open the door. We're police officers.'

Glass took a step to the side so that he was standing directly in front of the gap in the curtains and aimed his gun.

'No.'

I moved, but the princess was nearer and moved as fast. She went for Glass's arm, grabbing at it with both her small hands as he squeezed the trigger. There was an explosion, shattering of glass, shouting everywhere and the tall policeman falling to his knees on the gravel.

'No, don't kill him. No killing.'

She was formidable. He couldn't shake her off at once and that gave me a chance to move in. The princess and I attached ourselves one to each shoulder, trying to pull him away from the window. We might have managed it if one of the other men hadn't joined in to help him. Only one – the others were standing there watching, stupefied – but he was enough to tip the balance. Glass managed to pull away, went back to the window, fired again through the broken glass, once, twice. Then there was only a clicking sound. He swore and threw the gun aside in the general direction of the princess and me, missing us.

I ran to the window and looked out. Amazingly, both policemen were on their feet, running to the gate. The smaller one was still wearing his helmet but the other was bareheaded. A police helmet with a broken strap and a discarded truncheon lay on the gravel where he'd been kneeling. No blood, and from the speed he was making, no serious injury. The gate opened and they fell through it. Glass was pouring out obscenities, at the jammed gun, at us, at the other men for not helping him. I took the princess by the shoulders and guided her towards the door suggesting that we should leave him to it. As we came out to the landing Digby came out of the room next door and I realised that he must have been watching the whole thing.

'Two of them. What's the good of two of them? They never learn, do they? Never learn.'

'They'll be back with more.'

'Yes. The thing is, what are you going to do till then?'

TWENTY-ONE

AT THE BOTTOM OF THE stairs we met Violet and Veronica, white-faced.

'What's happened?'

I told them.

Violet gasped, 'He's gone and shot a bloody policeman?'

There were people behind them, in the corridor and the doorways of the dormitories. They'd have heard the banging on the door, the breaking glass and the shots upstairs, but hadn't seen the events on the front drive. A thin, high keening rose – the baby crying. This time Veronica didn't rush to comfort it but stayed rooted to the spot, staring at us. I explained that the policeman wasn't dead, not even injured as far as I'd seen. I didn't add that this would make no difference to our position, she could see that for herself. It might take Scotland Yard some hours to decide how to handle us, but the answer next time wouldn't be two unarmed police constables.

The added complication, that the basement was stuffed with dynamite and Glass intended to blow us all sky high rather than surrender, was something I didn't mention. I'd no idea how many of the commune knew about it, but suspected very few did. I thought that all of his miserable life had been directed to this day, when his hatred would burst in a climactic destruction that nobody could ignore. Fair enough for him, if that was what he wanted, but if the rest of us were involved as well, we should be allowed a vote.

Veronica said, 'We've got to get Serafina and the baby away before they come back.'

That was the thinking I wanted to encourage.

'I think we should all get away. There are enough of us here to lift that plank off the back gate. We walk away and keep walking.'

'Won't there be police outside?'

'Quite soon, I should think.'

If the two constables had any sense they wouldn't stop running until they reached their local police station, which was presumably linked by telephone to Scotland Yard. Even if the attempt to storm us didn't come until very much later, we should assume that we'd be surrounded.

There must have been at least ten of us in the corridor by then, around half the strength of the commune. A decision was made in the way group decisions so often are, not by discussion of ways and means but by a collective need to be somewhere else. Without another word being said we were all of us walking along the corridor and down the steps to the yard, with Veronica and myself at the front, Serafina and the wailing baby in the rear. The back gate was still barred by the great plank of wood and there were two men standing guard. I recognised one of them as a big surly man I'd several times seen speaking to Glass. Our party came to a halt a few feet away.

I said, 'We'd like to go out, please.'

No response. The surly man stared straight ahead, the other fidgeted. I suggested to Jimmy and the other strongest-looking men in our contingent that they should lift the beam off its sockets. Jimmy moved immediately, but the other man had only taken a tentative step when the surly man swore at him and he stopped. I looked round for Digby, but couldn't see him.

'Oh, for goodness' sake.'

Violet, Veronica and I went to the other end of the plank and, with Jimmy, started heaving.

'Stop that.'

Glass's high voice, from the direction of the house. We went on heaving. More shouts, the sound of running feet, then a shot banged into the thick wood of the door a few feet above our heads. We'd only managed to shift the plank a few inches, but when that happened it crashed back into its sockets.

Jimmy shouted, 'What the hell do you think you're doing?'

The answer was obvious. Either Glass had got his gun unjammed or he'd had a second one in store. He walked up to me, so close that he showered me with his spittle when he talked.

'We're not having any spies getting out. You're in it with the rest of us.'

Veronica faced up to him.

'You've got to let Serafina and the baby go. They haven't done anything.'

'The police would kill the baby anyway. Nobody's going.'

He took a second gun out of his pocket and handed it to the surly man. I was nearly sure that was the one that had jammed upstairs and that he wouldn't have had time to do anything about it. I made a mental note of that for use later if necessary, but meanwhile with Glass standing there with a gun that was certainly functional, we could do nothing. If the ten or so people in our contingent had rushed at Glass and the surly man, we might have achieved something. But the others were confused, easily cowed. Since at least some of them were on the run from the police too they might easily be persuaded that their safest course was to stay within the walls of the commune, even if those walls would be about as much use as rice paper if the police called in support from the army.

When he saw the doubt on their faces Glass gave a grin, like a gash in the skin of an overripe tomato.

'If you want something to do, you can go inside and start boarding up the windows. Tear up the partitions in the stables.'

Some of the men walked off, glad to be given a task. Jimmy Kelly looked at me. I think it was in his mind that he and I should make a dash on Glass together, but with even the possibility that the gun in the surly man's hand might be in working order, it was too dangerous to try. I shook my head. He took Violet's hand and walked her away towards the goat house. Veronica had to divert her attention to the baby. By now it had been yelling so long that its face had turned purple and Serafina was in tears too. She put her arm round Serafina and looked at me.

'I think I'll take them up to Sophia's room.'

'Yes, that might be as safe as anywhere.'

Not that anywhere in the house or near it could be considered remotely safe. We were like beetles in a matchbox in a schoolboy's pocket, with limited freedom to order our own affairs until the moment when he chose to throw us out or stamp on us.

I was on my own. Sounds of splintering wood and axe blows were coming from the stables. Glass looked at me, still grinning.

'See what happens to spies.'

Then he turned and went back into the house, holding the gun down at his side. I waited until he'd gone then walked through the archway into the kitchen garden. The hoes were there across the path, as people had left them before going into lunch, and the weeds cut that morning were already dying. The place seemed to be deserted and I couldn't see Digby anywhere at first. Then I heard a little rasping sound from the far corner behind the rhubarb and the gooseberry bushes. I pushed my way through young nettles and rampant mint and found him on his knees with an old chisel in his hand.

'What's going on back there?'

I told him about the deputation. He grunted.

'Wasting your time.'

I knelt down beside him and saw that he'd been scraping away at the mortar round a brick about five courses up from the ground. He pointed to the bricks below it.

'That lot are already loose, only I put them back for the look of it.'

'You must have been working on it for a long time.'

'Every hour I got, since I knew how things were going. If

we get another three or four out I reckon it might be just enough. I couldn't get through it, but you might. Good thing you're not too well padded – if you'll excuse my mentioning it.'

There was still this formality about him that nothing could shake.

'You must have been very good at what you did.'

I couldn't help saying it. An odd look came over his face.

'I tried. Whatever they might think, I tried to do my duty.'

He felt in his pocket and handed me a stubbier chisel.

'If you could start on that next one along . . .'

I knelt down and began scraping, head to head. It was strong Victorian mortar, hard to shift. I was impressed by the hard work and patience it must have taken for Digby to get so far.

'It's got to be big enough for all of them to get through.'

He stopped scraping for a moment.

'All of them?'

'All that want to go. You know about the dynamite he's got in the cellars?'

He nodded. 'I thought if you got out you might reason with them. Tell them there's women and children in here too.'

In my present status as prisoner on the run, I didn't fancy my chances of reasoning with the police force. Perhaps if I asked Geraldine to talk to the Home Secretary . . . but then, I'd have to get to her first through a hostile London.

'I think we'd better get as many of them as we can out together. How long do you think it will be before the police come back?'

He gave me a sideways look and tapped his knuckle against the wall.

'Could be here already.'

I looked at the wall, imagining a policeman a few feet away from us, and must have made some movement, because he laughed.

'What would you do in their place, always assuming there's somebody out there with a bit of sense?'

'They can't have a lot of sense or they wouldn't have just sent two strolling up to the front door like that.'

'Those were just the ordinary poor blighters sent to have a look at what was going on. They know now.'

'So what will they do?'

'What I'd do is send a lot of men up here quietly to surround the place, see that nobody gets out, only that will take some time because they'll have to bring them in from all the other divisions. Then I wouldn't move in until it's getting dark. More chance to take them by surprise that way, and get their nerves strung up while they're waiting.'

'So we've got till it's dark then.'

'Need to go before that.'

I lost all sense of time as we worked. Gnats rose and fell in the sunshine, blackbirds came to try the unripe gooseberries and chattered warnings to each other when they saw us, while we went on scraping at the mortar with blunt chisels. Now and again we'd talk to each other, but Digby wasn't a man who wasted words, apart from expressions of satisfaction when we prised another brick loose. We lodged them back, so that it would look on superficial inspection as if there was nothing wrong with the wall from the outside. Now and again feet tramped past in the lane, but there was no way of telling if they were police feet. After a while I ceased to worry and concentrated on finding ways of holding the chisel that would take the pressure off the worst blisters. My throat felt rough from the mortar dust, drier than the nymph marooned in the waterless fountain behind us. The sun was well on its way down, probably mid-evening, by the time we'd made a slot in the bottom of the wall large enough for an adult to wriggle through. Digby straightened up.

'Give it till the sun's down a bit more, then go.'

I waited on the inside of the brick archway until the guards on the back gate were looking the other way, then dodged around outhouses to get to the yard, so that nobody's attention would be drawn to the kitchen garden. The downstairs corridor was in almost total darkness, with even the stained-glass ship over the front door covered with planks. I heard a movement in the kitchen but it was only Turnip stirring in his sleep, hand round an empty plum-brandy bottle. I groped my way to the staircase and up to the landing and the door to the princess's room. The door was locked, but when I tapped on it with my knuckle there were movements inside.

'Who's there?'

I identified myself and Violet opened the door. The thick curtains were drawn over the windows, with planks nailed across them, and the only light came from a few candles in saucers that highlighted pale faces like fish in a dark aquarium. There were Sophia, Veronica, Serafina with the baby, all turned anxiously in my direction. Talking in whispers, because I'd no idea if Glass was in the room next door, I explained about the hole in the wall.

'For all we know the police are waiting on the other side of it, but it's a better prospect than staying here.'

If Veronica and Sophia had resisted I'd have told them about the dynamite, but the atmosphere of fear in the house made them ready to try anything. Still in whispers we arranged that they should go first, taking Serafina and the baby with them. If anyone tried to stop them, they should explain that the baby needed fresh air and they were taking it for a walk in the garden. Once there, through the wall and take their chance. Violet and I would follow ten minutes or so later, managing the excuses as best we could. We held open the door for them and heard them going down the stairs, Sophia saying something to a man in the passageway, then the back door opening and closing. Violet and I looked at each other and took a deep breath, then her hand came out and clutched mine.

We stood there, not saying anything, until I judged that ten minutes were up.

'Ready?'

'I'm not going without Jimmy.'

'Where is he, then?'

'By the front door, I think. That man with the squint came round and said all the men had to be by the front or back doors for when the police tried to come in.'

'How are we supposed to find him?'

'We've got to, that's all.'

We went down the stairs. At the bottom she said quietly, in the direction of the front door, 'Jimmy?'

'Shh. Here.'

I'd been practically treading on him. He must have been sitting there against the wall. Violet hissed at him to come on, and the three of us made for the back door. It looked light outside after the darkness of the house, but the sun was down behind the wall and dusk probably not more than half an hour away. One of the men on the back gate shouted something to us. We walked on, not replying or looking round, and reached the brick arch, where Violet had a chance to look properly at Jimmy.

'What have you been doing?'

One eye was closed and red and his nose had been bleeding.

'I wanted to get down to the basement, have a look what was going on down there. A couple of them didn't like it.'

'Was Glass one of them?'

'No. He's probably down there already.'

Digby was sitting on the ground behind the gooseberry bushes.

'No one outside yet.'

'Have the others gone?'

'Yes.' He stood up and pushed a folded paper into my hand. 'Don't hang about. I reckon . . .'

Violet, helped by Jimmy, was sitting on the ground and gathering up her skirt ready to wriggle through the hole in the wall. There was a shout from the archway towards the yard, an incoherent noise but the point of it seemed to be that we should stop. It was Glass's ally from the back gate, the one with the gun that might or might not work. Jimmy swore and jumped up, but Digby took him roughly by the shoulders and pushed him down again.

'No, you help her.'

Violet, head already through the gap, was wriggling the rest of her body through and didn't look as if she needed help, but Digby's push was a strong one. He strode away, crushing mint and rhubarb under his boots. Polished boots. He'd found time, somewhere in all of this, to wipe off the dust of the mortar. I watched him walk up to the man in the archway, heard him ask what the trouble was.

'Nell, come on.'

Jimmy's voice, from the ground. I took a last look at Digby's upright back, more or less dived through the hole we'd made and was dragged to my feet by Violet waiting on the other side. Still no sound of a shot. Jimmy followed almost at once. As soon as his head was on our side, before the rest of his body followed, he asked me a question from down there among the weeds.

'Do you still think I shot that fellow?'

'No. I know who shot him.'

Then we were all three on our feet and running along the stony lane, gasping and stumbling. With no real sense of direction and the dusk coming down we ran until the lane stopped dead against a low wall. Over it, pushing and dragging each other, into the backyard of a dairy. Out of it, in a clattering of milk cans and the neighing of the milkman's horse from its stable, into a tree-lined street that looked as if nothing ever disturbed it except leaf-fall. All the time I expected to hear the sound of police whistles, of shots, but there was silence except for our running feet. Our street was heading for a junction with what looked like a main road. There was a sound from it of a motor vehicle hauling itself uphill. We pressed ourselves back against a privet hedge and waited to let it go past. It was a black motor lorry, moving slowly but with a reptilian sense of purpose. Another one came after it, then another. We counted five in all, moving uphill in the dusk with lamps on the front of them like the eyes of short-sighted beasts that go mainly by smell. 'I wouldn't move in until it's getting dark,' Digby had said.

Violet's hand was clutching mine again.

'Is it . . . ?'

'I think so.'

She took a long, shuddering breath.

'What will happen to them?'

I said nothing. I knew anything I could do would be useless against what was happening, but that was no excuse. I dragged my hand away from Violet and ran towards the moving column.

'Nell, what are you doing? Nell, stop. Stop her.'

At the vehicles' grinding pace I could easily outrun them, even in my awful shoes. I got level with the leading vehicle, outpaced it by fifty yards or so then ran out into the road ahead of it, signalling it to stop. I must, I suppose, have been waving the piece of paper Digby had given me. With no room to swerve round me it stopped reluctantly, yards away. I could hear the sound of brakes as the other vehicles stopped abruptly behind it, then there were policemen all round me, pushing me aside. I picked out the one who seemed to be in charge and tried to explain, about most of them being harmless, probably no more than one gun that worked, the basement full of dynamite.

Whether I'd ever have made sense to them I don't know, but it didn't make any difference because other police must have got there before us. While my group were pushing me out of the way and I was trying to make them listen there was a shock to the air that felt like a punch in the chest, then a roar and a sudden silence, followed by a tinkling fall of glass that seemed to go on for a long time. When I looked back to where we'd come from there was the glow of a fire against the dusk, probably much like the coronation bonfires of a few days ago. I got into the police vehicle without further protest, still clutching Digby's piece of paper. In the light from a police lantern I saw that the address, in upright and respectful handwriting, was much as I'd expected: To the Commissioner of the Metropolitan Police.

TWENTY-TWO

'IT WAS THE BOOTS,' I said. 'In that whole place he was the only one who'd polish his boots every day, so the burn marks would be covered up.'

We were in a square and tidy office high up in Scotland Yard. It was mid-morning, with the traffic noise coming up from the Embankment through a half-open window, an occasional seagull looping past. Up in the Strand the news placards would be full of the anarchist outrage in Muswell Hill. There were two men facing me across a long desk, an assistant commissioner and, inevitably, Inspector Merit. I was beginning to think I should propose him for membership of a translators' guild, since they seemed to call on him every time they needed to make sense of me, but he didn't look as if he'd have appreciated it. I'd delivered my letter the night before then slept in a cell at Scotland Yard, as unconsciously as the planks I was lying on.

'He was a very orderly man. A dutiful man too. It wasn't entirely his fault he'd been put in a position where he had to shoot Robert Withering.'

'He didn't have to shoot him.'

The assistant commissioner sounded tired. He was thin of face and sparse of hair.

'Perhaps not, but the alternative was letting him blow up this building and most of the people in it. You should pity the man. After all, you sent him there to infiltrate himself among the anarchists.'

'Did I?'

'Your Special Branch did. You might ask Mr Brust. I'm

sure he knows all about it. It's a hard thing to ask a man to be a spy. Not surprising if his judgement started to go. He'd had enough of the secret life. When he heard what they were planning to do in Whitehall he must have thought it was his chance to come out in the open, make an arrest there and then while they were insulting the king and disrupting the traffic. He was the kind of man who'd respect the king – the traffic too, come to that.'

'But it didn't happen in Whitehall.'

I sighed. I'd done my best to explain the night before, but it had all been tiredness and confusion. Perhaps I'd even been a little tired and confused myself.

'That was the diversion. Most of the people preparing that float thought it was simply some kind of anarchist charade, the mock execution. Only Withering and Glass knew the truth.'

And Veronica, but I hadn't mentioned her. She might have got away or for all I knew she might have been in the police cell next to mine.

'Digby managed to take somebody else's place, under that axeman's hood. I dare say when he was supposed to be cutting off the king's head in Whitehall he'd have torn off his hood, come out in his true colours and arrested the lot of them for breach of the peace.'

The assistant commissioner put his head in his hands. Inspector Merit was doing his familiar skin-stretching act.

'Only it was much worse than that. Almost at the last minute he found he was on a cartload of dynamite, heading for Scotland Yard itself, and the man beside him was striking matches to light the fuses. He must have knocked the matches out of his hand and started the fire accidentally. I don't know if he'd been given a gun, but Withering would certainly have one. Digby could have grabbed it from him in the confusion. After that he had only seconds to decide what to do. He thought the choice was made for him. He was an outlaw, poor man.'

'Outlaw?'

209

'He'd certainly exceeded his instructions. I don't suppose you give your men *carte blanche* to shoot anarchists, do you? Especially old Etonian anarchists.'

No answer to that. I hadn't expected one.

'He'd lost everything. He'd be dismissed from the service, on trial for manslaughter at best. Intolerable for a man who believed in order like he did. So he had only one purpose left. He knew there was a man back at the commune even more dangerous than Withering had been, and it was the last duty of his dutiful life to deal with him. So he went back – and he did it.'

I was sure that both Digby and Glass had died in that explosion. What nagged me was the question of how many others. I wanted to know that before they locked me up again.

'Assuming that your theory's right . . .'

The assistant commissioner began wearily.

'Assuming! We don't have to assume anything. It's all there in his letter.'

The letter he'd been so anxious I should deliver. Digby's apologia.

'That letter was no business of yours.'

'No business of mine?' I was furious. 'Did you think I'd simply carry it like a good little postman and not read it?'

I'd read it in snatches on the mad career back into town after the explosion, by wavering police lanterns, in a few seconds of light from street lamps, but I could almost have recited it by heart.

'Anyway, even without the letter you must have known some of it. You aren't denying, I suppose, that Digby was a police agent?'

Silence.

'Brust knew. I think he guessed that first night that something had gone badly wrong. Perhaps that was why he was so eager to arrest somebody for it – even poor Simon Frater.'

Inspector Merit gave me a look as if begging me not to start that again. From the moment I'd reached Scotland

210

Yard the night before, and at regular intervals since, I'd repeated my demand that Simon should be released and exonerated. If not I'd see the details got out somehow even if I had to spell it out in whitewash on Holloway roof.

'Have you released him yet?'

The assistant commissioner shifted in his chair and spoke to the wall, not looking at me.

'Certain procedures are in progress.'

'Have you released him yet?'

My shout brought a uniformed policeman looking in to see what the trouble was. Merit waved him away. I noticed that he was looking at his senior officer with some curiosity. When the assistant commissioner spoke again, the muscles in his cheeks were throbbing with strain.

'May I remind you that you are hardly in a position to hector me?'

'I don't need any reminders of the position I'm in.' My unwashed clothes, those shoes, reminded me of that with every breath and at every step, if nothing else did. I was beginning to hate him for his clean shirt. 'What about your position? Have you considered that?'

'My position?'

'You're a very senior officer in a force that employed a spy who went out of control. It's entirely due to his efforts – and a little fortuitous help from me – that this building isn't a mass of rubble by now. A person was shot a few hundred yards from where we're sitting. Your officers not only arrested the wrong man, they arrested me for trying to point it out. If I hadn't managed to escape from Holloway to sort it out for you, Simon Frater would have gone on trial for murder and you'd never have known what happened at the commune. I don't like my position, but it's a better one than yours.'

There was silence for a while after that, except for two pigeons scuffling on the sill outside.

'On the subject of your escape from Holloway . . .'

211

He had his cheek muscles back under control now. Time for revenge, and all the battalions on his side.

'. . . you are aware that escaping from prison is a serious offence, not to mention assault on a prison officer?'

'Of course I am.'

Five years? Ten years? I wanted to know, but couldn't ask him. I felt sick when I thought about it.

'Then there's the question of aiding and abetting another prisoner to escape.'

I said nothing. No point in going into who had done the aiding and abetting, or the undoubted complicity of Misery Minny.

'Have you any idea of the present whereabouts of Violet White?'

That was the first good news. At least she hadn't been recaptured yet.

'No.'

'Did she go to Muswell Hill with you?'

'Violet White is no responsibility of mine.'

'If you're concealing anything about her, that's another serious offence.'

'I've told you, I've no idea where she is.'

I hoped she and Jimmy were in touch with his friend with the shipping line contacts.

'What about a foreign woman called Anna?'

'Anna who?'

'She won't give her other name.'

'What does she look like?'

The assistant commissioner glanced at Merit, who supplied a recognisable word picture of the Anna I knew.

'Why do you ask?'

The assistant commissioner was opening his mouth to say it was no business of mine, but Merit got in first. He knew, at least, that he had to bargain.

'She was arrested last night with a group of suspicious foreigners on a tram in Highgate.'

'A tram?'

'They had no money to pay their fare and the driver

called a constable. The woman called Anna punched him in the face, so he called in reinforcements and arrested the whole pack of them.'

'Good.'

'You're glad?'

'Glad they survived.'

I was prepared to bet that Turnip would be one of them. Anna, who missed nothing, must have tracked our escape through Digby's hole in the wall and decided to use it for herself and friends. Loyalty to Glass had stopped short of mass suicide.

'Did the Anna woman have anything to do with the attempt on Scotland Yard?'

'I arrived there several days afterwards, remember. How would I know?'

Anna had enough problems without my adding to them. Still no mention of Veronica or the princess.

They went on for some time, asking about the commune and the people in it. I told them a little, without going out of my way to be helpful. No point now. After a while the assistant commissioner rang a bell on his desk.

'What happens now?'

'You'll be going back to the police cells for the present. Later you'll be charged with escaping from prison, and probably several other things as well.'

'As many as you can think of, you mean?'

The muscles in his cheeks were twitching again.

'That's out of my hands.'

I leaned back in my hard chair, pretending to relax.

'Ah well, it should be an interesting trial.'

'Why?'

'You'll have to let me speak in my own defence, won't you? It should make an interesting story for the press. I hope you'll look after that letter from Digby. We might need to subpoena it.'

His mouth opened a little. A glazed look came into his eyes, the unmistakable symptom of officialdom trying to digest a new idea. His mental juices were still lapping at the edges of it when the constables arrived to take me back to the cell downstairs.

It was a long miserable day and I try to forget it. Sometime late in the afternoon the door opened with the familiar prison clatter and crash and I was taken to a small room with Inspector Merit inside it. He looked as worried as usual and invited me to sit down.

'I thought you might like to know, they've been searching the rubble all day at that place in Muswell Hill.'

'Yes?'

'They've found remains of two bodies at least. I'm not going to invite you to identify them, because they're in pretty bad shape, but we've had one of our artists prepare this.'

He held out a sheet of paper to me. It wasn't a very good likeness, but then I hadn't seen what was left for the artist to work from. Recognisable, at least.

'That's Glass.'

'We thought it might be. We already had a file on him as thick as an encyclopaedia, but no picture.'

'And the other body? I take it you didn't need a drawing for that.'

'No.' He looked down at his hands on the desk, then up again.

'You're right. It was Digby.'

He sighed, then we were both silent for a while.

'What about his widow? Will she get a police pension?'

'You would ask that, wouldn't you? In the circumstances, I think the answer would be no, but there is no widow. No family at all that anyone knows about.' Another silence then, 'He seems to have been a lonely sort of man.'

'And a brave one. But I don't suppose there'll be any posthumous medals for Digby, will there?'

He shook his head. 'I think the kindest thing anyone could do for Digby would be to keep quiet about him.'

This seemed to me a low blow.

214

'That's all very well, but if you expect me to go to prison for five years or whatever they give people who escape from Holloway and not defend myself, that's asking too much.'

'I told them it might be. Of course, I'm not empowered to make any promises . . .'

'I see. All the promises are supposed to come from me, none from you.'

'As I said, I'm not empowered to make any promises or deals, but you'll notice there isn't a charge sheet on this table.'

'So?'

'Let's suppose that if you were to go back to prison for the thirty days the court sentenced you to in the first place . . .'

'It was an unfair charge in the first place.'

'. . . for the sake of keeping our records straight, so to speak, there might not be another charge.'

'Provided I keep quiet about Digby?'

'I didn't say that.'

'It was what you meant, though?'

A nod so infinitesimal he could deny ever making it.

'One more thing, though, if we're keeping the record straight.'

'Yes?'

He looked wary.

'It's twenty-five days left, not thirty. I've already served five of them.'

He sighed. 'You drive a hard bargain, Miss Bray.'

'I need to. So how will your beloved records explain my temporary absence from Holloway?'

He massaged his face into something like a smile.

'I suppose we'll have to regard it as coronation leave.'

215

EPILOGUE

I WON'T SAY THAT twenty-five days soon pass in the circumstances, but they pass. In due course I found myself walking down the hill from Holloway with my own clothes on my back, my own shoes on my feet and the dusty summer air flowing into my lungs. This time there'd been no welcoming committee at the gates, as after more conventional suffragette incarcerations. That came as a relief. Given the way Emmeline felt about me at that point, if she'd sanctioned anything it would probably have been on the lines of a lynch mob. Even half the story, which was all she'd ever hear from me, would confirm all her worst fears.

Still, after a few days of doing nothing in particular, I did find my way back to the familiar office in Clement's Inn and friends who, even if full of concern and curiosity, didn't overwhelm me with questions. Besides, we had work to get on with. We always had. Simon Frater had been at liberty for three weeks by then, with as much explanation and apology as one usually gets from the police, which is to say not very much. They accepted, reluctantly, that he'd never intended to fire at the police on the bridge and gave him a stiff but superfluous lecture on the dangers of firearms.

He, of all people, was owed the full story so I told it to him in his cluttered little university office with the bust of Julius Caesar on the windowsill. He was grateful for the story, but I noticed he'd developed a wary way of looking at me, as if he expected me to summon up whirlwinds and

216

carry him and his papers away to God knows where. It took months for that look to wear off. I couldn't blame him.

In what time I could spare from catching up with my work, I tried to find out about the others. Max Blume with his network of contacts was a great help there. Princess Sophia got clean away. By the autumn she'd turned up in Paris, running a soup kitchen for pauper children under one of the bridges over the Seine. Max could find no mention of anybody with her who sounded like Veronica or Serafina and it was months before we got news of them. They were both in West Wales, where they'd joined a weaving co-operative making knobbly wool rugs under impeccably socialist conditions. What about the baby? I asked Max. Which baby? he said. According to his source of information the co-operative was full of babies. I'm sure that one of them was the offspring of an Italian girl and an anarchist of good family and Veronica will see it does well. Anna got six months for assaulting a police officer, which was fairly lenient in the circumstances. Our paths didn't cross in Holloway and I made no attempt to keep in touch afterwards.

Violet and Jimmy got safely to Australia. I know that much because she managed to get a message to me by very roundabout means. Don't worry about them, she said, because it was a good country and Jimmy was a man in a thousand. They'd see me again one day. I'd like to have known more, but it's a big place and I don't imagine that either of them has much time for writing letters.

Michael was the one who puzzled me. I was almost sure that with his capacity for tragedy he'd have managed to die there in the ruins of the commune at Muswell Hill. I searched the back numbers of the papers when I came out, but there was no reference to a third body. Then, quite a long time afterwards, I saw him at a concert in London, at the back of the ranks of second violins. He didn't look happy, but then it was a Wagner night. I wondered whether to go round and re-introduce myself afterwards, then decided that he wouldn't want to be reminded. He'd almost certainly found another woman to make him unhappy by then.

In due course I paid Misery Minny the fifty pounds I owed her. I had plenty of better things I could have done with the money, but I supposed it was a debt of honour in its way. I traced her to the dress-making place she ran with her sister-in-law in Islington and the money changed hands on the pretext that I was ordering a new winter wardrobe. In acknowledgement one dress arrived, harsh green wool with stitching as puckered as her mouth. I gave it away.

Oh, the horse that pulled the cart. I inquired after it when I met Inspector Merit by chance one day outside the Houses of Parliament. He sighed as usual and said he knew I'd get round to asking that, so he'd made it his business to find out. Sold to a grocer in Wapping with a reputation, I'd be glad to know, for treating his animals kindly. Was I keeping well? He was delighted to hear it. Then he walked smartly away, as if he feared I'd get him into trouble if he stayed there long enough. It was only after he'd gone that I remembered I'd meant to ask about the goats as well, but I expect they survived as goats usually do.